E.H.

W9-BGI-438

Tomahawk Meadow

This Large Print Book carries the
Seal of Approval of N.A.V.H.

TOMAHAWK MEADOW

A WESTERN STORY

LAURAN PAINE

THORNDIKE PRESS

A part of Gale, Cengage Learning

Detroit • New York • San Francisco • New Haven, Conn • Waterville, Maine • London

GALE
CENGAGE Learning®

LIBRARY OF CONGRESS CATALOGING-IN-PUBLICATION DATA

Paine, Lauran.
    Tomahawk meadow : a western story / by Lauran Paine. — Large print ed.
        p. cm. — (Thorndike Press large print western)
        ISBN-13: 978-1-4104-4646-6 (hardcover)
        ISBN-10: 1-4104-4646-8 (hardcover)
        1. Large type books. I. Title.
PS3566.A34T64 2012
813'.54—dc23   2011048800

Published in 2012 by arrangement with Golden West Literary Agency.

Printed in the United States of America
1 2 3 4 5 6 7 16 15 14 13 12

TOMAHAWK MEADOW

I

It was one of those situations a man sometimes rode into without warning, without expectation, and without any desire or taste for. The range men fired a volley just as Buckner's horse turned up out of a dusty, bone-dry cañon, and the sound startled Buckner as much as it surprised his horse. They hunched toward the top-out because they were already committed to the extent of this trail, but the moment they got up there where foggy dust lay here and there and where men were locked in a fierce little savage battle, they both wished they were almost anywhere else.

It was easier to make out the range men than it was to see their adversaries, but in this territory at this time Ladd Buckner had no doubts about the identity of the wispy, raggedly firing people across the arroyo-scarred grassland in among the thin stands of pines. In fact, when the range men seemed to be in the act of converging, in the act of mounting their common effort and peppered the first and second tier of trees, several of those bushwhacking individuals, stripped to moccasins, clout, and sweatband, whisked back from tree to tree in a shadowy withdrawal. They were Apaches, which meant they were also Ladd Buckner's enemies. They were in fact the enemies of everyone, even including certain subdivisions of their own nation.

Buckner swung off, drawing out the Winchester as he stepped to the talus rock soil, then turned his horse out of the cleared place in the direction of the trees, and sank to one knee as a bronco Apache swung free and darted up an exposed stretch of highland trail, racing for cover. Ladd Buckner fired, along with four or five range men who had also been awaiting just such an opportunity, and the fleeing man turned over, headfirst, like a ball and rolled into a tree where he unwound and lay sprawled and lifeless.

Another pair of bronco Apaches suddenly turned back, and Buckner, who was on higher ground than the other range men and for that reason had a better sighting, tracked the lead Indian and fired. The Apache gave a tremendous bound into the air as though bee-stung and lit down, racing harder than ever. Among the range men someone shouted encouragement in a pleased voice. Buckner tracked the second Apache, and fired. That time he'd held slightly downhill instead of uphill, and the Indian's legs tangled, then locked, and he fell in a limp heap.

Finally now the Apaches had guessed they had an enemy on their right flank where they had expected no one, and began cat-calling back and forth as they attempted to shift position, but the range men were after them now like hawks. The stranger's arrival and deadly shooting had completed the necessary unity among the bushwhacked range men; they systematically fired at every movement up along the foremost ranks of spindly forest, keeping the attacking Apaches on the defensive.

A man's powerful, deep voice sang out in English: "You up there . . . keep watch! They'll get behind you if they can! Keep down . . . keep low!"

Ladd Buckner heard without heeding. He knew as much about Apaches as any of those range riders down yonder. He was not worried about himself; he was worried about his horse. Apaches would kill a man's horse if they possibly could, although they much preferred stealing it.

But this time it appeared that the Indians had had their belly full. In a space of minutes when they'd had no reason to think it possible, since this had been their careful bushwhack, they had lost two warriors, shot dead on their feet, from a direction that their previous scouting had shown them there was no danger. The range men began hurrying, finally, passing up along the gritty bottom of an arroyo, booted feet grinding down hard as they hastened ahead, knees bent and never straightening as they came on toward the nearest stand of pines. They had been caught completely unprepared by the first Apache volley, and they'd taken a couple of casualties, but that momentary surprise did not last and now the range men, coldly and mercilessly angry, were going after their attackers. They made such good progress that a brace of broncos who had boldly — and foolishly — advanced well ahead of their companions to jump down into one of the arroyos and attempt a stalk closer to the range men could hear them coming. The range men made no attempt to be silent; they talked and cursed and scuffed dirt and stone and rattled gun stocks along the sides of their arroyo. They did every careless thing that to Apaches was a sin, but they kept coming and eventually the Apaches could no longer remain in the arroyo.

Ladd Buckner was straightening around after having brushed some belly-gouging sharp small stones from beneath him when the first raghead appeared, head and shoulders like a rattler lifting more and more and more as they twisted left and right. Ladd held fire. The Indian jumped out of the cleft in the grassland and turned up across the open territory in a desperate race for the upland shelter where his tribesmen were already withdrawing. Ladd settled the gunstock closer, snugged it back until it became almost a part of his slowly twisting body, and was ready to fire when the second bronco sprang up out of the earth and also began wildly running. It was a distraction but only a momentary one, then Ladd fired.

The foremost Indian gradually slackened pace. He seemed to want to continue to rush along but the harder he tried the slower his gait became, until the other bronco ran up and without even a glance shot past and kept right on running. From far back a number of range men sang out, then an immediate ragged volley ensued. The unhurt, swiftly speeding buck went down and rolled end over end. His uniquely

11

slowing, stumbling friend was not fired upon. The range men, like Ladd Buckner, lay there frankly interested in just how much longer the wounded buck could keep up his charade. Not much longer. He stopped, legs sprung wide, used his Winchester for a support, and turned very slowly to look over where Buckner had fired from. He could not see the man who had hit him but he tried to locate him. Then his knees turned loose and he fell, first into a sitting posture, then he rolled over.

The Apaches had failed in their attempt at a massacre that would have provided them with horses, pocket watches, pistols, and shell belts as well as cowboy saddles that brought a great price deep in Mexico. The reason they had failed had simply been because someone who could shoot accurately had appeared suddenly over where there was not supposed to be anyone, and he was still over there, prone in the rocks. As the broncos withdrew, wraith-like into their shadowy world, one bitter man went back and aimed into the talus where Buckner was, and fired. The slug ricocheted like a furious hornet. Buckner pressed lower than ever and tried to find that Indian. He never succeeded.

The bronco sent in another probing shot,

doubtless hoping to come close enough to make Buckner move, but he was not dueling with a novice. Buckner felt the sting of stone without moving any part of him except his eyes. He tried as hard to locate his adversary as the bronco did to locate him, and the end of it occurred when the range men got up to the northernmost end of their arroyo and suddenly, recklessly sprang out and raced for the nearest trees. The Apache had to end his manhunt and race up into the shadows in the wake of his retreating companions.

The range men blazed away where there were no targets, which was not as futile as it sometimes appeared. Apaches could be anywhere, prone under leaves, up trees watching for stalkers below, or even stealthily coming back to fight again. They weren't. They had failed, and, although the numbers were equal, they did not fight pitched battles. It was not their way and never had been. They were specialists in ambush, in stealthy mayhem, in wispy comings and goings. By now, wherever they had hidden their horses back upslope, they would be springing aboard to haul around and race away. Their casualties were already forgotten. At least three were dead, which they could not have helped but notice, but that bronco Ladd Buckner had shot down last was wounded. Still, the broncos did not have room, or time, for chivalry. If a man dropped, wounded or simply out of air or perhaps just stunned, he was counted a fatality because the enemies of the Apaches rarely took prisoners. The Apaches did not take them, unless they were half-grown children, and neither did their enemies.

Those charging range men burst past the first tier of trees, red-faced and in full throat. They wanted blood. In their environment there was no such thing as a worthwhile Apache. If they could have got up where the broncos had their tethered horses, they would have killed every man jack of those Apaches. It was hot out upon the grassland; that meant it was even more breathless in the humid foothills; those range men unlike their foemen were not accustomed to running on foot, and the Indians had achieved a speedy head start.

The gunfire ended, and after a while even the futile chase ended. The Apaches had disappeared, so the range men turned back, whip-sawing their breath, shirts plastered flat with salt sweat, their legs and hips aching from the mad charge up from the grassland into the spindly forest. They cursed between deep-drawn breaths and

14

tried to guess which way the ragheads had gone so that perhaps later on they might be able to go in pursuit. Until they were low enough again to see beyond the forest's fringe to the range beyond, they seemed to have forgotten that man over in the talus rock who had so perfectly confused the Indians by appearing on their right flank with his deadly gunfire.

"Whoever he is," a youthful, wispy, tall rider said, "he sure as hell deserves a medal."

"Came up out of the cañon just before the fight started," stated an older man. "I seen him. I figured, by God, he was another raghead, except he had a white man's way of settin' his horse and all. You're dead right . . . he sure come up out of there in the nick of time."

"We'd've cleaned them out anyway," grumbled another man.

"Yeah, most likely," conceded the older rider. "But he came up out of there and sure made a hell of a lot of difference."

There was no way to dispute this statement even if the other riders had wanted to dispute it, which none of them did. Then they came out of the trees and saw Ladd Buckner squatting beside that wounded bronco, and angled off in that direction. The sun was high, the air smelled of burned powder, and far out several saddled horses grazed peacefully along.

II

Buckner was not an exceptionally tall man. He stood six feet, and in heft weighed about twenty pounds less than a couple of hundred, but if this amounted to an average man in physical respects when the three range men ambled up and halted as Ladd Buckner arose from beside the wounded Indian, it became clear to the observing survivors of that raghead ambush that Ladd Buckner was something more than simply a range rider who had inadvertently come down out of the northward hills and up out of that gravelly cañon at the precise best moment for him to appear upon Tomahawk Meadow.

A dark-eyed, black-haired, stalwart man shoved out a soiled hand and said: "I'm Chad Holmes, range boss for the Muleshoe cow outfit. This here is Buster Dent, Jack Caruthers, and Pete Durbin."

They pumped hands once, then let go, and Chad Holmes looked long at the unmoving, snake-eyed Indian on the ground whose middle had been bandaged. Then

16

Chad turned from the waist to look else-where and said: "You fellers better see if you can catch those damned horses, and, if so, you'd better tie Morton and Devilin across their saddles." As the cowboys turned away, Muleshoe's range boss turned back for a more thoroughly assessing study of Ladd Buckner. "You sure came up out of that cañon at the right time," he said.

Buckner sounded indifferent as he replied: "Mister Holmes, I'd have given a lot to have been ten miles easterly in some other cañon, but once we started up out of there, we didn't have room to turn around to head back down."

Holmes looked at the Apache again. "Where did you hit the son-of-a-bitch?"

"Through the body," replied Buckner. "It's one of those wounds you don't know about until some morning you look at him, and he's stiff as a ramrod or else he's grin-ning back at you."

"He isn't going to grin," said the dark-eyed range boss.

Ladd hooked thumbs in his bullet belt and considered Muleshoe's range boss. Chad Holmes was dark, 'breed-looking, stalwart, and physically powerful. He was about Buckner's age, thirty or thereabouts, but he was thicker and not quite as tall. Muleshoe had plenty of reason to hate this particular raghead. Most northern Arizona range men had abundant reason to despise most Apaches.

Ladd Buckner also had reason to hate ragheads, but, although he understood exactly how the range boss felt, he was opposed to murder even when it was committed against ragheads, so he said: "Mister, this one belongs to me."

Holmes shot a dark glance upward. "What does that mean?" he demanded.

"I saw him, I fought him, and I shot him. I also patched him up. He belongs to me. That's how they call their shots."

"Yeah, but we're not ragheads," stated the range boss. "This son-of-a-bitch was in a bushwhacking band and I got two dead cowboys to prove it. We got laws about something like that."

Ladd sighed. "You don't lynch this one, mister."

Holmes began to look less baffled than antagonistic. "You're going to stop the four of us?" he quietly asked. "What's your name, mister?"

"Ladd Buckner. No, I'm not going to stop the four of you, Mister Holmes, I'm only going to stop *you*, because you and I are the only ones standing here." Buckner paused, traded looks with the 'breed-looking Mule-shoe boss, then gently smiled. He had a very nice smile. "Mister Holmes, I don't deal in favors, but this time I guess I got to. I did you boys a little favor coming up out of the cañon when I did. Do you object to settling up small debts?"

Chad spat aside and glanced again at the venomous-eyed, prone Apache. "All I got to say to you, Mister Buckner, is that, if you insist on being foolish over one stinking rag-head . . . all right. Just don't be around here when my riders come back because they aren't going to stand for this, if you're still here." He looked sulphurously upward. "What in the hell sense does this make? You're risking your life keeping one of those underhanded, treacherous bastards alive. You patch him up and the minute he gets a chance he'll slam a knife to the hilt between your shoulder blades."

Buckner disputed none of this. He knew Apaches as well as anyone else knew them. "If he gets behind me, it'll be my own darned fault," he told Chad Holmes, and looked up and around. "You know, Mister Holmes, I was on my way southward to a place called Piñon when I came up out of that blasted cañon. How much farther is it?"

"Twelve, fifteen miles," stated the range boss. "It's our nearest town. In fact, it's the only town anywhere around the Tomahawk Meadow range country." Holmes assumed an interested look. "You acquainted down there?"

Ladd wasn't. "No, sir, but I read in a newspaper up at Cache Le Poudre about a harness works being for sale down there."

Holmes dryly said: "Mister, if you can sew a trace or rig a saddle as well as you can shoot, I'd say you'll make a fair living in this territory."

The Indian attempted to sit up and Chad Holmes turned stonily to watch. Ladd Buckner stepped back and set a big leg behind the bronco for support. It was a rough but a generous gesture. The Indian settled back and glared. "Subbitch," he snarled at Chad Holmes.

Neither of the range men moved nor replied. Far out one cowboy had managed to catch one of those loose saddle animals and was now astride it going in search of additional stampeded saddle horses. It would be inevitable that some of the loose stock had not stopped after being abandoned when the Indians had first struck. By now those horses would be two-thirds of the way back to the home ranch of Muleshoe.

Ladd Buckner leaned to hoist the wounded Indian up to his feet. Chad Holmes, arms crossed, stood and watched. If the raghead's life had depended upon some merciful act by the range boss, there would have been another dead Apache.

Ladd encircled the Indian's middle with a strong arm and turned to head in the direction of his saddle animal. Chad remained, arms crossed, bitterly watching, but he did nothing to interfere.

Buckner had to waste time because the wounded Indian sagged badly a couple of times. When he got to the horse, eventually, the Indian looked back and grunted.

The Muleshoe men were clustered around their range boss. They were mounted, but there were no spare horses. That meant the two dead cowboys would have to make the trip to the home place flopping behind someone's cantle.

Ladd propped the Apache against a sickly pine with yellowing needles, held the reins to his drowsing horse, and waited a long while leaning upon his Winchester. But the range hands did not come. Maybe Holmes had given an order that the men had obeyed, or, more likely, he had not given any order at all but had simply pointed out that Ladd Buckner was no one to fool with, if he chose to oppose them, and they did not need any more casualties, certainly not over one lousy raghead who was probably going to die anyway.

The Muleshoe men turned off southwesterly after loading their dead men and rode off without a rearward glance.

Buckner continued to wait. The Indian watched him and seemed to get weaker as the moments passed. By the time Buckner thought it was safe now to head out, the Apache weakly held aloft a hand and wagged his head.

"No good," he muttered in mission English. "No more good for me."

Ladd knelt, leaned aside the Winchester, and pulled back the bandage he had created from the raghead's shirt. There was almost no external bleeding, but the flesh around the point of entry of the perforating bullet was turning a bad shade of blue. It was not as noticeable on the Indian's hide as it would have been on a hide with less basic pigment, but it was still clear enough. There was no swelling, though. Perhaps there would not have been swelling in any case since the bullet went into the man's mid body in the soft parts and emerged out of his back the same way, in the soft parts.

Buckner put the bandage back in place

and said: "You give up awful easy, Apache. I've been hit harder than that in the mouth and never even stopped talking."

The Indian was sick, which he had every right to be, but it amounted to more than a reaction to being injured; he was also demoralized and beaten. His type of people died very easily, almost handily, when these conditions combined against them.

Buckner went to his saddlebag and returned with a pony of brandy that he poured into the dull-eyed Indian. The Apache choked and almost gagged, then his eyes copiously watered, but their brightness momentarily returned, and, as he panted, his stare at Ladd Buckner remained quizzically bleak but interested. He clearly could not imagine why a range man would go to this trouble over him.

Ladd stoppered the pony and hunkered opposite the Indian as he said: "Now listen to me, strongheart. We're going out of here, you on the horse, me walking ahead of it. Do you understand what I'm saying?"

The Indian understood. "I ride, you lead."

"Yeah. Now tell me where your people are, because I can't take you down to the cowman's town and I'm not going to sit around up here in among the trees for a couple of weeks until you can make it on

23

your own. You tell me, and I'll take you pretty close to where they'll find you, then we'll part. You understand?"

This time the Indian said: "Why?"

Ladd considered the bottle he was holding. "Because I don't like murdering folks. You wouldn't understand." He arose and glanced over both shoulders. The land was totally empty as far as a man could see in three directions. It was probably equally as empty northward back up through the forest but there was no way to be sure of that since visibility was limited to the first tangle of trees.

The Indian jutted his chin. "Cowman go there," he gutturally muttered, indicating the southwesterly distance Chad Holmes and his Muleshoe men had taken. Evidently the Apache knew this territory well enough, and evidently he thought Ladd Buckner would be interested in where the nearest ranch might be.

Ladd did not care in the least where the Muleshoe Ranch was. He leaned to hoist the Indian. Without a word he roughly reared back and boosted the Apache across his own saddle. The Indian locked his jaws and fumbled for the saddle horn, then held on with his face averted. He was in great pain.

Ladd did not replace the Winchester in its saddle boot. It was another burden to be shouldered as he walked ahead, leading the horse, but close to fainting or not, that raghead up there was still capable of making a murderous effort. They skirted around the nearby cañon and angled up into the foothills where the muggy heat was noticeably oppressive, and once the Indian almost turned loose all over and fell, but Ladd caught him, swore at him, and roughly straightened him up again. Then he handed up the pony of brandy, waited until the bronco had taken down two more swallows, and struck out again.

Finally the Indian dripped sweat and got light-headed, so Ladd had to rest beside a deep little narrow creek. Here, he upended several full hats of cold water over the raghead, and, when the Indian recovered and was able to be moved again, Ladd asked where the Apache *ranchería* would be.

The bronco would not confide in him. He simply pointed vaguely and said: "Put me down four, five miles. Put me down out there."

Ladd used up the last of his brandy getting his ward ahead that far, but he made it just ahead of full darkness, and, as he eased the bronco down and was leaning over, he said — "Good luck, you murderous son-of-a-bitch." — and swung up over leather to retrace his way back down toward the grassland again.

He had no feeling of having done a Christian deed, if indeed that was what it had been, since an awful lot of non-Christians had done similar things. All he thought of as he picked his way through the darkness to the last of the uplands and emerged back upon the rangeland was that he'd done what he'd felt needed doing and that was the end of it — and from now on, when he came up out of a cañon in the Tomahawk Meadow countryside, he would look first before he rode right on out.

III

They were having a *fiesta* of some kind the day Ladd Buckner reconnoitered Piñon, then rode on in and put up his horse at the livery barn. There was a lot of that reedy kind of lilting Mexican music over in the cottonwood grove east of the town plaza, which usually went with celebrations in the Southwest. At the livery barn all a little bandy-legged oldster had told him was that one of those traveling troupes of pepper-belly play actors had driven into town the

26

night before last and had set up their stage over between Mex town and the business section of Piñon. It did not have to be a *fiesta* then at all.

It was late in the day. Ladd needed a bath, a shave, and a place to stay, and he was in no big hurry, so he went first to a café opposite the jailhouse for a meal, and after that he walked the roadway on both sides, familiarizing himself with the town of Piñon, and finally he strolled to the shaded front of the harness and saddle works to stand out front, hands clasped loosely behind him, and gazed at the manufactured goods on display beyond the wavery glass window. The work was excellent. In fact, even people who did not appreciate the full expertise of the Piñon harness maker would have been impressed. Whoever he was, he was no novice; he had not been a novice according to Ladd Buckner's guess in perhaps forty or fifty years, and this was not only the truth, it also happened to be the reason he had his harness works up for sale.

An open-faced, tousle-headed young cowboy walked up, leaned to see what Ladd was admiring, and amiably said — "Sure is the best, ain't he?" — and passed southward without awaiting a reply.

Ladd stepped to the doorway, but the

shop was locked. There was no one at the workbench or behind the counter inside. It was not really that late, but evidently this particular merchant thought it was, because he clearly had closed up shop for the day.

Across at the saloon there was a spindly little coming and going, mostly it seemed of townsmen who were coming from the direction of the Mex music and play acting, as though perhaps whatever play was being enacted over there induced thirst. Ladd went in search of the hotel and found that Piñon had instead a boarding house. He got a room, then paid an extra two bits for a chunk of tan lye soap and a scorched old towel. He followed the arrows to the bathhouse carrying his one and only change of attire from the bags on the saddle he had brought up with him from the livery barn. Bathing was always work, unless a man did it in a creek, and then it was usually uncomfortably cold. At least this time he got warm water from the great brass kettles atop the old cook stove, and could draw the cold water by pulling a corncob out of the hollowed log that served as a pipe from some distant spring.

When he was clean and freshly dressed and even neatly shaved, he hung the gun and belt around his middle, emptied the

28

tub, and trooped back inside with the towel and soap. Darkness had settled. Piñon was ready for one of those fragrant, bland summertime nights, and the Mexican musicians were at it again over at the cottonwood park east of town where nearly all local celebrations and *fiestas* were held.

He had a drink at the saloon, then ambled over where light from a long row of guttering candles at the foot of an improvised stage helped him select which vacant seat among the hand-squared big old cottonwood logs, arranged in ranks like benches, best suited his requirements. He did not have to get as close to the footlights as some men did; he could see well enough from midway back. And it was awfully hot down that close to those burning candles. Nor did anyone actually have to get that close anyway, unless they wanted to. There was a full moon this night.

Mexican urchins passed soundlessly back and forth on bare feet showing vast smiles as they sought to sell pieces of candy — chunks of squash soaked overnight in brown sugar water. Several cowboys who had already made too many trips back to the saloon were behind Ladd making remarks about the buxom leading lady, a sturdy woman in her thirties with a magnificent downy mustache, who swooned into the arms of the hero at regular intervals, but only after he had got his legs braced. In fact, as Ladd sat there eating his chunk of candy watching the performance, he noticed that the tall, handsome hero of the play in his elaborate but not very clean soldier's uniform knew exactly when the buxom woman would throw herself at him. The hero began preparing himself moments in advance. Even then, several times she made him stagger.

The musicians were exceptionally gifted. The difficulty arose from the fact that, although they never once left their darkened places beyond the lighted stage as most of the male audience did, from time to time the musicians kept getting out of tune and off-key as the evening advanced. They had bottles of *pulque* and tequila discreetly cached close around where they sat.

The plot of the drama had to do with the buxom lady's enormously difficult struggle to retain her virtue against the lecherous machinations of a rather portly civilian twice her age who knew every way to achieve his dastardly ends. She wavered between yielding, and rushing into the arms of the heroic soldier who was her true lover but who kept going off to join in wars and

30

revolutions, until, near the end of the play, with all the participants perspiring profusely as a result of the heat generated by all those candles, the buxom heroine was finally caught out by the evil, leering, portly villain. In her subsequent despair, self-loathing, abysmal agony and anguish, she used up the entire third act that culminated in her suicide.

Ladd had another piece of the sugar-soaked squash and wandered away from the cottonwood grove. But most of the other spectators lingered until the final act when the big woman plunged a shiny dagger into her ample cleavage, and sank with many outcries and lamentations to the stage at the feet of her heavily perspiring soldier lover. She required almost a full five minutes to expire, during which the portly villain, standing just out of the candlelight in gloom and shadows, leered and dry-washed his hands and chuckled, something that prompted all the Mexicans in the audience to hiss fiercely at him. A number of the non-Mexican audience also joined in and some-one hurled a carrot that missed but that nonetheless inspired the villain to move back a little farther into the shadows.

Ladd finished his candy and rolled a smoke while standing near a huge old cottonwood tree where a number of other men idly stood. One of them said: "Last year someone fired a shot over his head" — meaning the villain — "and the troupe was mad as hell next day because they could not find their villain for the next play."

Ladd grinned and looked at the speaker. He was a graying, tall man with a droopy mustache and a nickeled badge on his shirt-front. As Ladd lit up, he said: "That lady's pretty stocky to be hurling herself into the arms of the general . . . or whatever he is."

The lawman agreed. "Yes. She's been piling it on for the past three, four years. I recollect her first performance here in Piñon. She was a slip of a woman. Well, the Mex taste runs to hefty ones." The lawman looked around with a wry twinkle. "I sort of agree with that myself. I just never cared much for mustaches, though."

They grinned together, then Ladd wandered off back in the direction of the town's main business area. It was a very pleasant night, and probably because it was midweek there did not appear to be many range men in town. Maybe that helped the town remain calm and relatively quiet and peaceful.

A man driving a dusty top buggy rolled past with his little lamps lighted and merrily glinting. The man had on a dented plug hat and a rusty old frock coat. There was a small black leather satchel visible upon the seat at his side. He was a somewhat stocky individual, round-faced, and not very old-looking. He saw Ladd and nodded as though they were acquainted, then kept right on rolling in the direction of the livery barn.

Southward and upon the east side of the road there was a small office sandwiched between two larger buildings with the legend *Doctor Enos Orcutt* upon the window in elegant gold letters. Ladd guessed that had been Dr. Orcutt who had just driven past. Not many other occupations required a person to haul a little leather satchel around with them. Also, plug hats seemed to go with the frontier medical profession.

At the saloon a snub-nosed, red-faced, bull-built older man brought Ladd's beer and nodded genially at him as though he knew a stranger when he saw one and was perfectly willing to welcome strangers to Piñon. His name was Joe Reilly and at one time he had been a career soldier, but a musket ball at Antietam had cut short that career, something Joe had sworn up and down ever since was the best, and most painful, thing that had ever happened to him. Perhaps because there was not much trade right at the moment he lingered at Ladd Buckner's end of the bar to talk a little. When Ladd explained who he was and why he had come to Piñon, the saloon man grew warmly expansive. It seemed that Joe Reilly was by nature an accommodating, friendly man.

"It's the rheumatics," he explained, "that made old Warner put his works up for sale. Some days it's so bad he can scarcely close a fist. Other days he can sew a harness tug without any pain. He told me just a couple of days back that if he couldn't sell out directly, he'd just have to hold an auction, then head on out to his daughter in California." Reilly was also interested in Buckner's ability. "You been a saddle maker long, then?"

Ladd replied without sounding as though he felt a compulsion to explain: "Best way for me to demonstrate, I expect, would be to work a few weeks with Mister Warner. All the bragging in the world wouldn't make me a harness maker, would it?"

Joe smiled. "You're right. And in these parts, Mister Buckner, folks judge a man by what he can do, for a fact."

Ladd said: "It's a nice town. Pretty and all . . . with trees and flowers."

"We got water," stated the saloon man.

"That's what makes the difference, you know. A town can have the prettiest view and the nicest settin' and the friendliest folks, and without water it's nothing." He could have added "especially in Arizona" but he didn't, probably because anyone who knew anything at all realized that water, or rather the shortage of it, had always been Arizona's biggest dilemma. "You'll like folks hereabouts," stated Reilly, who had been in the Piñon country for eleven years now.

"How about Indians?" asked Ladd mildly, and Reilly's geniality vanished in a second. "Them lousy sons-of-bitches," he boomed. "Yes, we've got 'em. Sneakin' little murderin' raghead scuts, they are. They can steal the horse right out from under a man without him knowin' it, they can. Slit throats of fellers who are lyin' in their bedrolls. They're the curse of the territory, Mister Buckner. I got to admit we got 'em. Wouldn't be honest not to warn folks against the bandy-legged little mud-colored bastards." The matter of Apaches usually brought up a related subject in the territory. It did now, with Joe Reilly. "And the bloody Army!" he exclaimed. "What does it do, I'd like to ask you? Not a darned thing, that's what. It goes chasing Mex horse thieves all over the countryside, and doesn't even

35

acknowledge the ragheads. I tell you, Mister Buckner, when I was soljering, we looked at things a lot different. In those days we'd hunt them down and scrub them out down to the nits. Nowadays the Army's soft and riddled with politics."

As soon as the saloon man paused for a breath, Ladd moved in swiftly to change the subject. "What time does Mister Warner open his harness shop in the mornings?"

Reilly had to wait a moment until his adrenalin diminished before replying. "Oh, I'd say about eight o'clock. Yes, usually about eight. I see him over there about then."

Ladd paid for his beer, smiled his thanks, and left the saloon carrying away with him a critical bit of local lore. Never mention Apaches around Joe Reilly unless you wanted to be skewered to the bar front while Reilly got it all out of his system.

IV

Three weeks of sleeping on the ground followed by one night of sleeping in a boarding house bed seemed to signify a change in the lifestyle of Ladd Buckner. When he went forth in Piñon the following morning, early, and walked both sides of the town before heading in the direction of the café, he was beginning to feel that he belonged, and yet he hadn't even known Piñon had a bank until he paused in the new day chilly dawn light out front of a square little ugly red brick building to read the sign: *The Stockgrowers' Trust & Savings Bank of Piñon, Arizona Territory.* There was someone's name beneath all that fine lettering but Ladd looked in at the barred windows ignoring the name, then continued on his way to the café.

Five or six laborers were already at the café counter, wolfing down breakfast, and one of them who was called Abe by the others had a magnificent black eye that was the unavoidable butt of all kinds of rough comments among the others. Evidently they all knew one another. It was impossible for Ladd to believe those other men would have teased the man with the black eye if they hadn't all been friends, especially since the man with the black eye stood better than six feet tall and weighed well over two hundred pounds.

The café man did not come for Ladd's order. He instead brought coffee and a platter of steak, hashed spuds, and a piece of warm apple pie. The pie in particular was unbelievably delectable, and yet to look at the slovenly café man it was hard to believe he could have made such a thing.

An older man arrived, sat next to Ladd, and, as he reached for the tinned milk to weaken his coffee, he winced and exasperatedly said: "God damn rheumatics."

Ladd handed over the tinned milk and gazed at his neighbor. The man was at least sixty and in fact probably was seventy years old. He was tall and gaunt and scarred. His hands were stained and work-roughened. Ladd said: "You wouldn't be Mister Warner, would you?"

The old man finished washing down his coffee, then looked over. "I'd be," he admitted.

Ladd introduced himself and smiled. "I been on the trail three weeks getting down here after seeing an ad you had in a newspaper up north."

The old man's eyes brightened. "Is that a fact? About the harness works?"

"Yes."

"Well, well," stated old Warner, and pushed out a hand. "Shake, son, then we'll finish eatin' and walk across the road." Warner reached for his knife and fork. "You married by any chance?"

Ladd wasn't. "No, sir. I'm single."

"That's good," stated the harness maker,

"because the shop'll make a decent livin' for one person, but it won't support no woman, too, and no kids." Warner studied Ladd a moment as he chewed. After he swallowed, he asked another question. "You got enough real money to buy me out?"

"Depends on how much you got to have," stated Ladd.

"Well . . . five hundred dollars?"

Ladd took his time about answering. He drank coffee, hacked at his breakfast steak with a dull knife, looked around, then smiled at old Warner. "Kind of hard to eat and talk business at the same time," he murmured.

Old Warner had to be satisfied, then, until their meals were finished and they passed out into the new day sunlight. The town marshal was passing and unsmilingly nodded at them, his gray gaze flickering in recognition over Ladd Buckner. Across the road in the harness shop the smell was pleasantly familiar; it was an amalgam of tobacco smoke, new leather, and horse sweat, but mostly it was of new leather.

Old Warner puttered, handling tools, talking as he moved from workbench to cutting table to sewing horse and finally to the counter and the hangers where repair work hung, each article with a scrap of paper on it giving a name and a price in cryptic longhand. It required no great power of observation to see how difficult this day was for the old man. He had spent a major portion of his life here, good years and bad, wet years and drought years. He had buried a wife while operating this business, had raised two children, only one of which, a daughter, had survived, and from that front window he had watched dozens of friends he had known most of his life pass by for the last time.

Finally he went over to poke some life into a small cast-iron stove and to place a dirty old graniteware coffee pot atop it, and to remove his hat and scratch, then resettle the hat as he said: "What can you stand, son?"

Ladd had one thousand dollars in Union greenbacks in a belt around his middle. Five hundred of it was in old-style notes, five hundred was in later, and crisper, greenbacks. He said: "Mister Warner, I can't buy it and sell it, too. You put on a price, and, if it's too much, I'll just walk back out of here, and if it's not too much, we'll shake on it."

Old Warner was aged and lined and stooped but his eyes were as clear as new glass while he made his judgment, then said: "Five hundred dollars, Mister Buckner." He smiled a trifle sadly. "It's worth more, but

I'd a sight rather see you succeed than have to operate hand to mouth only to get cleaned out if a bad year hit the range and folks didn't come in very much. You keep back what you got to have to operate on and give me five hundred, and tomorrow morning I'll be on the stage to California."

They shook hands, then Ladd went to the workbench, reached inside his shirt to unbuckle and remove the money belt, and under the frankly interested gaze of old Warner he counted out $500. In turn, the harness maker wrote him out a painstakingly clear and inclusive bill of sale, then, after handing this over, Warner turned and looked around, and turned back with a grim-faced little nod.

"Treat it good, son, and it'll do as much for you. It's a fair and decent livin' and it's got a reputation for doing right by folks."

Ladd went out to the shaded overhang with the harness maker, feeling poignant and sad for the old man.

Warner turned and smiled as he said: "Good luck, son. Someday you'll come to this day, the same as I came to it, and I sure hope you can turn it over to the next young buck with a plumb clear conscience."

Ladd watched old Warner trudge northward in the direction of the stage station, watched him turn in up there, then he also turned and walked away, heading for his new business. He was experienced. He was a good saddle maker. In fact, he had more experience at saddle making than he had working up sets of harness. For a couple of hours, until the liveryman brought in four broken leather halters, Ladd examined the patterns and templates. The liveryman looked surprised. After a moment of explaining what he wanted done to the halters, he looked up with a squint and said: "You're the new harness maker?"

Ladd introduced himself. "Yeah. Mister Warner sold out to me."

"You're young," said the liveryman, who was not quite old Warner's age but who was fast approaching it.

Ladd smiled. "I'll hang around Piñon until I can remedy that," he said. "Tell you what. I'll repair your halters, and, if you don't like my work, you don't have to pay for it. Fair?"

The liveryman nodded. "Fair." He walked out without offering his hand or smiling. In a place no larger than Piñon where most residents had been there all their lives or at least for over a dozen years, newcomers were never viewed with frank delight, first off. Barring Joe Reilly, Ladd did not expect to be taken to the town's heart by its established residents until he had earned that kind of recognition. He was willing to work for it. He had his reasons for being willing to work for respect and acceptance. If even Joe Reilly had known the reason for his willingness to do this, Joe would probably have been just a tad more reserved in his association with Ladd Buckner. As it was, Joe got his first outside opinion of Buckner three days after old Warner had departed forever from Piñon, and the new saddle and harness maker was organizing his time and materials to turn out his first riding saddle as the newest businessman in Piñon.

Chad Holmes of Muleshoe rode into town with two of his cow camp men on the seat of a ranch wagon, and, while the rig was being loaded around back at the dock of the general store, Chad and his range men went up to the saloon for beer. There, Joe Reilly mentioned the new harness maker, only to discover that the men from Muleshoe already knew him. In fact, as the range men told the story to Reilly, Ladd Buckner was a dead shot with his carbine and one of the best fellows in the entire territory to have on your side in a skirmish with ragheads.

Joe inevitably broadcast this tale. Ladd

did not know the Muleshoe men had been in town. Neither Chad nor the others came across to the harness works to see him. The first Ladd knew that his episode on Tomahawk Meadow had finally reached town was when two teenage embryonic cowboys who lived with their parents in town arrived at the saddle shop one afternoon to stare and smile a lot, and finally to blurt out that they had heard Ladd was a professional Indian fighter, and that he had come along and had single-handedly routed an entire war party of Mescalero Apaches, the worst of the lot, with only his Winchester.

Ladd laughed, then came over to the counter to lean there and explain exactly what had happened out there, beginning with his own very strong desire to be anywhere else when he rode up out of the cañon and found himself in the middle of a fierce little gunfight. The boys left, finally, to spread the word that along with being probably the most formidable Indian fighter since Al Sieber, Piñon's new harness maker was also a man imbued with that most valued of all frontier ethics — modesty.

It all helped. Joe Reilly did his share, too, and whatever some people, most particularly womenfolk, thought of Reilly's profession, people were inclined to trust his judgment of humanity. Joe favored Ladd Buckner, so it became a lot easier for folks to smile a little, and to nod. The liveryman, too, admitted that old Warner hadn't been able to sew as well in years, when he got his busted halters back. "And he's makin' a saddle," stated the liveryman to his cronies out front in tree shade at the loafers' bench near the stone trough. "He's an honest workman. No danged copper rivets in the rigging. It's every bit of it hand-stitched and buckskin-threaded. That's how I tell an honest man. When he does something right, even when he knows it ain't going to show when he's through with it."

"But he's young," muttered one of the townsmen who regularly sat down there out front of the livery barn chewing cut plug and whittling on soft cottonwood chunks.

"Well, God dammit," stated the exasperated liveryman, "so was you, once, Al, although darn' few of us can remember it now. Anyway, give him enough time and he'll outgrow that."

"He'll probably raise the prices," grumbled another older man. "They all do. Let some new feller come to town and buy in, and the first thing he'll do every time is raise the blasted prices."

The liveryman had a retort for that, too.

"Tell you how I feel about that. He fixed up four busted halters for me and hardly charged enough to cover the thread let alone the time. I figure I'm that much ahead right now, so the next few times he could even charge me a mite more and I'd still be breaking even."

The other older men went silent and remained that way for a while about the new harness maker. Therefore, what possible good could come out of it if the liveryman, who was favorably impressed, continued in pressing this discussion? None, of course. Eventually one of the old men got back upon a topic that they never wearied of, and that they never agreed upon, either, but that they could discuss and swear about and denounce one another over without much danger of actually hurting anyone's feelings — politics.

No one else in Piñon cared a whoop about politics, and generally for a very good reason. They did not live in a state of the federal Union; they resided in a territory, and since all the territorial areas of the U.S. were administered by the Army, there was very little of the elective process to make politics interesting. Otherwise, of course, there were the national elections, but out in Arizona someone could run for President

and even be elected, and Arizonans would
not even know who he was for several weeks
after he'd moved into the White House. It
usually took that long for the news to reach
isolated cow communities like Piñon.

V

For Ladd Buckner there were a number of
concerns to take precedence over such
things as politics, and he was not, and never
had been, very politically aware. Like most
people out in the territories, living from day
to day with hardship, privation, and real
peril, politics like a lively social involvement
constituted a luxury. It would be a full
generation yet before the cow country
would be able to afford a socialized strata
or a politically active environment. Presently
as Ladd told Town Marshal Tom Wharton
when the lawman strolled in for coffee and
a visit one morning, perpetuating a habit he
had established fifteen years earlier with old
man Warner, if a person could just eat three
times a day, keep dry, and pay his bills, he
was probably doing about as well as folks
could expect to do in Arizona Territory.

Tom Wharton, who was quite a bit older
than Ladd Buckner, who had run the gamut
from Indian scout to buffalo hunter, to

47

range man and lawman, sipped coffee over by the stove and slowly nodded his head. "And keep out of trouble," he added, watching Ladd buck stitch a bucking roll. "Eat, keep dry, pay the bills, and keep out of trouble." He eyed Ladd Buckner thoughtfully. "You haven't met Doctor Orcutt yet, have you? Well, sir, he told me one time that it was his opinion that, if folks out here didn't get shot or snake bit or horse kicked, they'd probably live longer than the national average. It's healthy out here. The air is clean, the food is natural, the water's not bad from too many years of folks abusing it."

"Just keep away from ragheads," said Ladd whimsically. "Don't set in any drafts, and maybe mind your own business a little."

Tom Wharton sparingly smiled. He rarely smiled any other way. "You've got it about right." He watched the strong, deft hands working at the sewing horse. "You sew well," he said. "That's sure going to be one hell of a good saddle when you're finished with it. You know, when old Warner was younger, I didn't think there was a better man with leather in the territory. I'm beginnin' to figure you might be just as good." Marshal Wharton finished his coffee, rinsed the cup, and draped it from the nail above the cutting table where it had hung suspended beside old Warner's coffee mug for years. "I'll break the habit," he told Ladd, "if it bothers you to have a person bargin' in first thing each morning and having a cup of java. It's just that old Warner and I had that arrangement for many years, and now I got it as a habit."

Ladd looked up from the sewing horse. "Nothing's going to change very much in the shop," he told the lawman with a little warm smile. "I'll keep putting the pot on first thing, Marshal."

"Tom," said the lawman, winked, and strolled out into the sunlight of a new day.

Ladd had an opportunity to meet the man Marshal Wharton had spoken of that same afternoon when the medical practitioner walked in to have the grip on his satchel repaired. It had broken loose. As Dr. Orcutt said, they just didn't put handles onto things like they did when he was first in practice a number of years back. Then he laughed at himself. Up close, Ladd got his first good look at the doctor, and came to the conclusion that, although Enos Orcutt looked quite young, he was probably in his forties. Ladd also made another judgment of the doctor. Enos Orcutt talked and acted, and even looked like a man who marched to the cadence of his own drummer. It was a good judgment; if there was one thing Dr. Orcutt was known for around the countryside, it was an independent mind and manner. When other medical men were prescribing purgatives for appendicitis, Dr. Orcutt was applying ice packs and performing swift surgery. He left Ladd with a feeling that he would be a good man to put one's trust in.

When Ladd handed over the repaired satchel, the doctor said: "Perfect match for the first time it was ever done, after I bought the satchel up in Colorado, Mister Buckner. That time it lasted six years, the longest it's ever lasted."

Ladd smiled. "Doctor, try putting it down and lifting it up. No leather on earth can stand too much roughness."

Enos Orcutt smiled back, but skeptically. "Mister Buckner, in my business you don't always have time to put something down or lift it up. Sometimes you have to toss your satchel into the buggy, and sometimes you also have to yank it with you when you jump out of the rig. But I'll try. How much?"

"Ten cents," replied Ladd, and watched the doctor count out the small silver coins.

As Orcutt headed for the door he said: "You come from Colorado, did you?"

Ladd nodded, then puzzled a little over

that question. Why had the doctor asked it, and why hadn't he said Idaho, Oregon, Wyoming, or Montana? It did not matter. Ladd went back to do some of the repair work that had trickled in over the past week or so. He had learned long ago that the articles folks brought to be repaired were important to them on a day-to-day basis and the surest way to antagonize people was not to have their articles ready when they called for them.

The liveryman returned, this time with a woman's side-saddle that had slipped under a horse, had dumped its rider but without serious injury, although the agitated horse had proceeded to kick the saddle unmercifully until someone could control the beast and remove the outfit. Ladd looked at the remains without commenting, and the liveryman, who was watching Ladd's face as some sort of gauge as to what the repair bill might be, finally said: "It's genuine old Kentucky spring seat, Ladd. It'd be a blessed shame to toss it into the rubbish heap. They don't make spring seats any more."

Ladd avoided a definite commitment by saying: "Come back day after tomorrow." The reason he gave no commitment was because he was unsure of the actual condition of the tree beneath the leather. If the tree were still sound, then all he would have to do would be replace a lot of leather. If the tree were smashed. . . .

Tom Wharton, in one of his pre-breakfast morning coffee sessions, told Ladd how the accident had occurred that had resulted in the ruin of the side-saddle. "Darned kids walking down the alley with a big old yeller mongrel were pitching rocks for the dog to chase. They rolled a stone directly under the damned horse and it took to bucking. The *cincha* was loose anyway. The lady wasn't hurt." Tom's gray eyes assumed their near smile as he said: "Maybe she'll be eating off the mantel for a few days, though."

Ladd put the side-saddle upon a work-horse and showed Tom Wharton the extent of the damage. He also showed him how a genuine spring seat was constructed, and, although Marshal Wharton was interested, up to a point, in the articles of a trade that had been as much a part of his life as anything else, the saddle was a woman's rig, and Ladd Buckner discovered a probable reason for Tom Wharton's single status. He did not show the least interest in the Kentucky saddle because it had been made for women; he clearly did not have much regard for womenfolk.

"The father of the lad who owned the yellow dog," Marshal Wharton related, "was going to whale the daylights out of the dog. I stopped him on the grounds that the dog didn't do a blessed thing he wasn't supposed to do . . . which was obey his master. Then the damned fool was going to larrup his lad, and I stopped that, also. The boy had no idea the rock would roll under that darned horse."

Wharton sighed, refilled his cup, and stood, wide-legged, where he could see past Ladd across in the direction of the roadway window. Out yonder in the yellow-lemon summertime heat, roadway dust arose from the slightest motion, and as near as the far side of the road there were dancing heat waves. Full summer had arrived. There probably was no place on earth where full summertime could be as unnerving, as generally debilitating, as it could be in Arizona Territory.

"If I'd learnt a trade instead of always having to rush over and see what was on the far side of every blessed mountain," mused Marshal Wharton, "I'd probably right now be doing what you're doing, Ladd, and the good Lord knows it's a sight better than being a lawman." He paused to sip coffee, and to say it afterward exactly as he had been thinking it. "As an *aging* lawman."

Later in the day the foreman of the forge, which was near the south end of Piñon on the opposite side of the road, brought up a torn running-W to be repaired, and lingered to explain what had happened. It was a highly unusual horse that could not only survive a bout with a running-W, but that could break one of the things. This horse, according to the sweat-stained blacksmith, had not only broken the taming rig but he had also turned back, charged through the shop, put six grown men to flight, and had hit one old loafer with his shoulder, knocking him into the black water of the cooling barrel. The blacksmith smiled broadly. Ladd laughed along with the blacksmith. He promised to fix the rig so that it would not break again.

After the second week it was beginning to be predictable, how he would conduct the business, how much trade would come through his doorway, what the possible livelihood would net him, and, since the living quarters off the back of the little wooden building was his home and his only outside expenses involved supplies from Denver and an occasional drink across the road at the saloon, or breakfast and maybe supper at the café, he could pretty well estimate what the years up ahead held in store for him. Many men would never have settled for that. Many men would have felt stifled by the sameness of the routine and the predictability of the days, week in and week out. Ladd Buckner not only did not feel stifled; he settled into his routine with clear comfort and pleasure. And he was a good leather man. Even those skeptical old-timers who hung around the bench out front of the livery barn and who had for the most part been critical of every newcomer as well as every change and innovation ultimately decided after closely inspecting the new harness maker's work that he was not just good at his trade but that he was also a credit to the community.

Homage came slowly, but not as slowly as it could have come. Ladd accepted it like he learned to accept a lot of things in the Piñon countryside. Mainly he became passive because he had his work and he enjoyed every day of it. Other things could fit in, or not, as they chose, or as the people around him caused them to fit or not; he didn't care in particular, perhaps because as the weeks and days passed he became more and more aware that his work was approved of not only by the townsmen, the blacksmith, the doctor, and the liveryman, but also by the outlying cow outfits. He had repaired saddles, bridles, even boots and chaps, suspended all along one wall awaiting the irregular return trips to Piñon by men of the distant cow ranges.

Bert Taylor who owned and operated The Tomahawk Valley General Mercantile & Dry Goods Emporium was also Ladd Buckner's source of credit information, but as a matter of fact most of the people who brought in articles to be repaired, or who purchased new items, had a definite use and a need for them. Cow country was seldom where people defaulted on debts to merchants. Occasionally a cowboy would ride off and never return, or perhaps be killed out on the range somewhere, but harness makers rarely lost money. The repair bill on just about any saddle, bridle, pack outfit, or pair of boots never exceeded its saleable value. Ladd, in fact, made more money than old Warner had been making the last few years before he had sold out and left the country. The reason, according to Bert Taylor, whose store was across the way, was simply that old Warner's eyes had been failing him and his hands hadn't been up to the demands made upon them, with the inevitable result being that his work had suffered. Much that ordinarily should have come to Piñon went elsewhere to be rebuilt or repaired. Now it was beginning to trickle back to Piñon again.

Ladd was busy, and he was good at his trade, and once when Dr. Orcutt and Marshal Wharton came together at Reilly's bar for a nightcap, the doctor made a remark about someone as young as Ladd Buckner being as experienced and skilled at his trade being extremely rare, and Tom Wharton had leaned there, studying his empty shot glass for a long while before saying: "Enos, you don't just figure he's a natural leather man."

Dr. Orcutt agreed. "No, I don't. He sewed the grip on my satchel exactly the way a man from the Colorado penitentiary sewed it one time. I've only seen that kind of loop-through knotting done by men who've learned their trade in prison."

Marshal Wharton looked up with a sardonic, vague smile. "Funny you should say that, Doc. A while back I was over there, having coffee and watching Ladd work on a busted side-saddle. He made the identical routine moves a feller did I once sent to prison in Colorado, and who also learned his trade there, and came back to the territory years later, where I visited him in his harness works over near Tombstone. Funny we should both notice that, Doctor."

VI

Tom Wharton wrote to the authorities of the federal penitentiary in Colorado. It was a routine letter of enquiry by a man who was usually curious about people and things without ever being excessively interested. Wharton was pretty much of a live-and-let-live individual. But he was tough and thoroughly capable when he was required to be. He had that kind of a reputation and he had not acquired it by just talk.

When he had his morning coffee at the harness shop one clear, still, and azure early morning about a month after Ladd Buckner had taken over as harness and saddle maker, he had the reply to that letter he'd sent up to Colorado in a shirt pocket, folded neatly and buttoned out of sight. He made no mention of it. As a matter of fact for as long as Tom Wharton lived, he never mentioned that letter.

He stood and watched Ladd at work, and, when he'd finished his coffee and was ready to go forth into the rising morning heat, he turned at the door and said: "Ladd, Chad Holmes was by the jailhouse yesterday. We had us quite a talk. Your name came up."

The harness maker did not raise up from the cutting table but he lifted his eyes in a quizzical way. "He mentioned that little tussle at Tomahawk Meadow, did he?"

Wharton nodded. "Yeah, seems him and the other Muleshoe fellers are still talking about the way you handled that Winchester. They were also still talkin' about you holding back a hurt raghead. They wondered whatever became of him."

Ladd could understand that because he'd occasionally wondered the same thing. "I took him up within shouting distance of his *ranchería* and left him, and that's all I know," Ladd told Marshal Wharton. "I sort of figure he probably died. He was hard hit through the carcass."

The lawman was not convinced. "They're tough. They're tough enough to survive just about anything but a direct head or heart shot. I know, I've seen my share of 'em down a rifle barrel, and I've gone up afterward only to discover that the feller who was supposed to be dead had gone and crawled plumb away." Tom leaned in the doorway. Out in the roadway, northward to judge from the sounds they made, a number of horsemen entered town at a hard lope. Shod hoofs made a ringing sound over either rock or hardpan and this late in the summertime Piñon's roadway was purest hardpan. The lawman casually looked, then just as indifferently turned to gaze back where Ladd was leaning. "Muleshoe's making a legend out of the way you came up out of that cañon and busted into those ragheads like you was the cavalry." Wharton showed that vague, faint sardonic smile of his and straightened around to stroll away.

Ladd saw him take one step, then whip straight up in what looked from the rear as complete astonishment. He whipped straight up and hung there for perhaps five seconds, then he ripped out a muffled curse, and Ladd saw his body loosen, begin to settle flat down as Marshal Wharton went for his gun. Two carbines erupted. It sounded to Ladd Buckner as though one carbine was northward upon the opposite side of the roadway while the other carbine was on the same side as his harness works, but northward about as far as the stage station.

Tom Wharton went back drunkenly against the front wall of the harness shop, then loosened the grip on his six-gun, and turned very slowly with Ladd frozen in place, staring. Wharton continued to turn until he was staring straight at Ladd, then he turned loose all over, and collapsed in a heap.

Up the road someone sang out in a singsong sort of chant with his words being indistinguishable. Ladd pulled back, laid aside his cutting knife, wiped both hands on the apron, then reached back and systematically untied the thong, pitched the apron atop the table, and walked toward the doorway. He picked the six-gun from its holster upon a wall-peg just inside his shop, and walked out where the lawman was lying.

Up in front of the bank three armed men faced outward across the roadway with carbines cocked and held two-handed, ready. Another rifleman was indeed up in front of the stage station upon Ladd's same side of the road. Otherwise, the roadway was totally empty. Whether this happened to be a natural condition, or whether those two gunshots had emptied the roadway, was anyone's guess. Ladd studied the men at the tie rack out front of the bank, then moved slightly to step past Tom Wharton. Nothing happened. He saw all he had to see, up yonder, then slowly turned and gazed downward.

There was nothing anyone could do for Marshal Wharton. He had caught both of those slugs high in the body. He was either dead or within a breath of being dead. Ladd swung forward again, sank deliberately to one knee, and called ahead: "You at the tie rack!"

That was all; he simply called forth as though he meant to catch the attention of those men up there, and the next moment when one of those bank robbers stepped ahead to take his stance, Ladd shot him through the chest. The man fell, his carbine bounced against the plank walk, and those other outlaws swung to begin firing. Ladd was not the best target in the world, in shadows out of the bitter sunlight in front of his shop and beneath its overhang, but they could see him clearly enough if they made the effort, and they were certainly attempting to do that as they began firing.

It sounded like the Indian skirmish all over again. Gunfire built up to a fierce crescendo, then another of those horsemen up yonder dropped on his face, and the man over in front of the stage station suddenly panicked and raced as hard as he could over to join his companions out front of the bank. Ladd tracked this running man, aimed lower than before, and squeezed off a shot. The outlaw fell with a ripped-out scream, rolled and writhed with a smashed hip, then suddenly blacked out and flopped back with blood darkening his trousers and the dusty roadway around him. He needed immediate aid but no one offered to go out into the center of the roadway and give it to him. He died.

Two men darted from inside the bank. At the last moment one of them swung back around in the doorway and systematically fired. The echoes from within the brick building were deafening. Finally, now, there were other townsmen belatedly entering the fight, but it was over the moment the surviving outlaws flung up across saddle leather, sank in rowels, and raced wildly northward out of Piñon.

Ladd got to his feet, moved out to the center of the roadway, took two-handed aim, and emptied his six-gun without bringing down a single fleeing bank robber. Someone from Reilly's saloon darted to the bank doorway, halted, and yelled into the acrid-scented hush that followed Ladd Buckner's final gunshot: "Jesus, they killed 'em!"

People emerged, furtively and tentatively at first, peering up the roadway in the wake of the outlaws, and went over to join that horrified man in the bank doorway only when it was no longer possible to see the escaping outlaws because of their pillars of dun-colored dust up the stage road in the direction of the far-away hills.

Ladd Buckner remained out in the roadway, hatless in the violent heat and sun smash, shucking out spent shells from his six-gun. He had no other slugs to replace the casings with, so he walked back into the overhang shade where the lawman was lying, and knelt with the empty gun while he made a closer study of Tom Wharton. It had all happened just too fast. Wharton must have been the most thoroughly astonished individual in town when those bank robbers appeared and boldly fanned out to cow the town as their companions went inside to loot the bank. Wharton's death had also been too sudden and too thoroughly unexpected. Even the peaceful expression on his face had an underlying expression of total surprise. Sightless eyes stared up through Ladd Buckner and through the warped overhang ceiling above Ladd Buckner.

Enos Orcutt came out from between two buildings a few doors southward, did not speak, walked up, and sank to his knees, little patched black satchel at his side. Ladd pulled away, stepped inside to fish out six fresh loads for his useless six-gun, and re-armed the weapon while Dr. Orcutt went through his necessary but futile routine. Orcutt twisted to look up at Buckner as the harness maker slowly took down his belt and holster and buckled them on. "Are you all right?" the doctor enquired.

Ladd said: "Yeah, I guess they couldn't aim as well when someone was firing at them as they aimed when Marshal Wharton first got ready to brace them. He's dead?"

"Within moments of the time he hit the ground," confirmed Dr. Orcutt. "They cut him down as neat as marksmen cut them down back during the war. Like they were waiting for him to step out so they could do it."

Up the roadway someone began shouting for Dr. Orcutt to hurry to the bank building. Whoever he was he not only had a powerful set of lungs and a resonant voice, but he also had no intention of being quiet until Enos Orcutt appeared.

The doctor got to his feet and hurried forward, clutching his satchel, leaving Ladd Buckner standing there, looking a trifle quizzically after him. Why would the doctor say Tom Wharton had died as though those outlaws had expected Tom to step forth from the harness works, exactly as Tom did step forth. Orcutt had made it sound as though it were, in one way or another, a kind of prearranged killing. He had made it sound as though someone had deliberately set the lawman up to be murdered.

Joe Reilly and Bert Taylor came across from the opposite side of the roadway and stepped up into overhang shade to stand mutely staring. Reilly, the former soldier, said: "God damn, they nailed him right through the brisket. He didn't have a chance at all."

Bert Taylor lifted a troubled face to Ladd. "He didn't even get a chance to draw, did he?"

Ladd looked at the holstered Colt for the first time. "Doesn't look like it," he replied. "What did they do up at the bank?"

"Killed the head man and shot hell out of the cashier!" Reilly exclaimed. "My God, they didn't just come to town to rob us. They rode in to kill as many folks as they wanted to."

"Renegades," stated the storekeeper. "I can't believe it happened this way. There wasn't a word of warning. I was at my desk in the back room when the firing started." Taylor looked blankly at Ladd Buckner. "You turned them out. What else might they have done if you hadn't shot it out with them?"

"Nothing," said Buckner. "They got the money. That's all they came for."

"But . . . look at Tom," protested the storekeeper. "My God, look at what happened inside the. . . ."

"God dammit," snapped the harness maker, "I told you . . . all they came for was the darned money." He holstered the recharged six-gun and turned back into the harness shop, leaving the two older men out there gazing after him, until eventually they looked at one another and Reilly said: "Leave him be. It's darned upsetting, shooting it out like that."

They trudged back in the direction of the opposite side of the roadway where people were beginning to throng up in the direction of the bank's bloody and rummaged interior. It was a hot day; the raid had occurred shortly before noon; there was settling dust far up the stage road for a half hour after the attack, and for most of the residents of Piñon what had occurred had in fact happened exactly as the storekeeper had implied — too suddenly, too unexpectedly, and too swiftly for them to see any of it although all but the stone deaf had heard the gunfire.

The legends began even before the dead men had been hauled feet first down to the doctor's buggy shed for preservation until graves could be dug. Eventually Tom Wharton was also carried down there, and, during the subsequent course of Enos Orcutt's preparation of the Wharton corpse for burial, the doctor extracted that letter from the marshal's shirt pocket. He also read it.

VII

The outlaws were identified from dodgers in the late town marshal's office as three members of a renegade gang that normally operated farther southward, down closer to the international border. Bert and Joe Reilly composed a letter to the Texans and the New Mexicans who had worked up those dodgers, informing them that three of the wanted men had been shot to death at Piñon, Arizona Territory, and gave the date of those killings as well as the circumstances surrounding them. Then they put in requests on behalf of Ladd Buckner for the bounty money and neglected to tell Ladd that they had done this. It was a plain oversight; neither Taylor nor Reilly had experience as lawmen. They only did what had to be done, then they went among the other townsmen to urge the appointment of some kind of interim committee, or perhaps a vigilance organization to keep the peace and enforce the law until a new lawman could be appointed. None of it was precisely according to the law, but all of it was according to the community's immediate needs and desires.

Dr. Orcutt embalmed the three outlaws and Tom Wharton, then one evening he came down to the harness shop after closing hours and pummeled the door until Ladd emerged from his rear quarters to admit the medical man. Orcutt had three separate bundles, pitifully small and woefully insignificant. He offered the bundles to the harness maker, and, when Ladd suspiciously pointed to the counter top, Enos put the bundles up there.

"Everything which was in the possession of those three outlaws you shot," he told Ladd Buckner. "But there was actually nothing much to be used to identify the men." Enos shrugged and leaned upon the counter. The only light in the shop was coming through the rear doorway that led into the harness maker's living quarters. "There are pictures of two of them among the flyers Tom kept at his jailhouse office, and an excellent description of the other one," Enos Orcutt added. "They were vicious, unprincipled sons-of-bitches, Ladd, if that makes you feel any better."

Buckner changed the subject. "Care for some coffee? I just made a fresh pot out back in the kitchen."

Enos shook his head and continued to lean and study the younger man. "You're not troubled, then, about having killed those three men?"

Ladd's expression flattened a little, smoothed out in an expression of cold, unfriendly regard of the medical man. "There isn't any way to kill people and not be troubled, Doctor. Even men like those three. But if you mean . . . has it ruined my appetite or did I lose sleep, or have I begun to fear retaliation from their friends or kinsmen . . . the answer is simply not one blessed bit." When Orcutt was about to speak again, Ladd held up a hand to silence the older man. "But there is one thing that's been bothering me, Doctor. You said while you were on your knees beside Tom Wharton that it looked to you as though someone had given a signal or something when he stepped out of my shop, that he had been shot down deliberately like maybe it had been planned that way."

Orcutt did not drop his gaze as he replied to what sounded very much like an accusation. "That's roughly what I said, indeed. Ladd, he was hit twice. You could place a playing card over both those holes, they are that close and that deadly."

"What of that?"

"Ladd, all those men fired at you and they didn't even come close enough to nick you."

Buckner scowled. "You'll have to make it plainer than that, Doctor."

"Well, how would it have looked to you? Wharton walked out of your shop into the shadows under your wooden awning, and there was no reason for those outlaws up in front of the bank to expect him to do that, or to know he was the law, or even to see him in that shade the way they did at that distance. But, Ladd, they were completely ready, as though they were expecting him to appear and had their guns ready. Tom was shot down methodically. That is the only conclusion I can come up with. I've written it up in my medical report that way."

Dr. Orcutt continued to lean and gaze at the younger man for a while, then he slowly hauled upright and fished in a pocket, brought out a crumpled, much-folded piece of paper, and shoved it across the counter toward Ladd Buckner.

"Read that," he said. "It was in Tom's right-hand shirt pocket when I prepared him for burial."

It was the letter from the prison authorities up in Colorado and Ladd Buckner only read the letterhead and the first couple of paragraphs, then he slowly replaced the letter upon the counter top. "You believe I was somehow involved in that bank robbery?" he asked in a voice made reedy by his own incredulity.

Dr. Orcutt looked at his hands for a moment. "I don't see why, if you knew those men were going to raid our bank, you would have deliberately sent Tom out to be shot down, and then why you would have followed him out to shoot it out with those renegades." Orcutt raised his eyes. "Unless you are a homicidal maniac, Ladd. Unless you are the kind of human being I cannot possibly understand." He pointed to the letter lying between them. "You served seven years in the federal penitentiary in Colorado for bank robbery. . . . There is the whole record in black and white. And just in case you need to know how Tom got interested in your possible background, we both noticed that you stitched, knotted, and sewed exactly the way the rehabilitation people teach their pupils to work at the prison up in Colorado."

Ladd glanced again at the letter, this time at the date it had been sent. "How long had Wharton had this information?" he asked, and the doctor did not know except to surmise that, since the letter had been dated two weeks earlier, and the usual mail delivery required only one week, that perhaps Tom Wharton had had that letter at least a full week.

Ladd was doubtful. "He didn't so much as even hint about what he knew when he came in for coffee each morning."

Orcutt conceded that. "You didn't know Tom as well as some of the rest of us knew him. He wasn't a man who would use something like this to hold over your head, and he never would have intimidated you with it. He would just keep it in mind, and, if you never forced him to make a case against you, he would never have mentioned it." Dr. Orcutt's voice changed slightly, turning brisk and more incisive as he went on. "But he's dead, and so are a number of other people including our bank president. Maybe the cashier will die. It's too early to determine that."

Orcutt paused and Ladd, who was certain there had to be more coming, leaned there, waiting.

"If we had enough time maybe I could say this diplomatically," averred the medical practitioner, and ruefully smiled a little. "Although I've never really had the knack for diplomacy."

"Say what?" asked Ladd.

"Say that there is an old saying, Ladd. It

73

takes a thief to catch a thief. We no longer have a law officer. No one I can think of offhand has your ability to face guns and to use them as well as you can."

Ladd stared. "Me? Are you asking me to go after those renegades?"

"I'm asking you on behalf of the town council, which includes Reilly and Taylor and myself, to do something like that. The alternative is for the town to send out to the cow outfits for volunteers, and by the time they arrive back here those murderers will be out of the country. . . . It's your town, Ladd. You came down here, set up in business, and adopted it."

"And a member of the town council believes I had a hand in the murder of Piñon's lawman."

"No," stated Enos Orcutt, "I at no time said I believed that. I said it looked as though someone had set Tom up, and I still think that may have happened. On the other hand he could have simply walked out there coincidentally. Ladd, we can discuss this anytime, later." Orcutt reached to pick up the letter lying between them and fold it. "Right now we have some dead men to avenge by law, and we have an awful lot of money, mostly the savings of folks around town, that needs to be recovered, and we need your help to accomplish those things." Orcutt slowly pocketed the letter without taking his eyes off Ladd Buckner. "I'm making an appeal. You can refuse."

Ladd nodded in the direction of the pocket Enos had just used. "Sure, just an appeal . . . and, if I don't help you, the letter will be circulated around town."

For a moment longer Enos Orcutt stood motionlessly, then he reached, withdrew the letter, tossed it over in front of the harness maker, and said: "Burn it, if you want to, do with it whatever you want." He started to turn. "I'll be down at the livery barn with the others saddling up, if you change your mind."

"What others?" asked Ladd.

"Joe Reilly and Simon Terry, the blacksmith."

Ladd scowled. "That's all. Just the three of you?"

"Well, no, we were kind of figuring there would be a fourth fellow," said the doctor, and walked on out of the shop.

Ladd looked from the empty doorway to the letter, picked it up, and read it, then balled up the letter and crossed over to pitch it into the little iron stove. He got his booted carbine and his belt weapon with its shell belt. He took his time about rigging out, and, when he moved across the room to pick his hat off the antler rack near the workbench, and a hostler from down at the livery barn walked in carrying some torn chain harness, Ladd pointed. "Dump it in the corner there," he said, then, booted carbine across one shoulder, he herded the liveryman back outside. The hostler offered absolutely no objection. He looked from Ladd's face to his weapons, then scuttled southward without a word.

Several cowboys were just stepping to the ground from their saddles up in front of Reilly's place. Ladd saw them without being the least bit interested. Elsewhere, as he walked forth, then turned back to lock his roadside door, he also saw those two gawky teenage pseudo-cowboys who had questioned him one time about the fight at Tomahawk Meadow. He ignored them, too, but they certainly did not ignore Ladd Buckner, who was armed to the teeth and who looked bitter-faced as he swung to hike southward down the roadway.

Apparently Dr. Orcutt had told his companions something about his conversation with the harness maker, because, although Joe Reilly would have normally been his customary loquacious self, this time, when Ladd appeared, all Reilly did was look up, nod his head, then look down again as he finished rigging out his saddle animal.

Dr. Orcutt was back nearer the wide front barn opening. He had been watching the northward roadway so Ladd's appearance did not come to him as a surprise. He allowed the harness maker to get close, then he casually gestured toward the burly, dark, and bearded man. "Simon Terry," he said by way of a curt introduction. "Simon, this is Ladd Buckner."

The blacksmith shook Ladd's hand in a grip that could have crushed bones, then unsmilingly went back to saddling and bridling his animal. Simon Terry was a powerfully muscular man, dark as a half-breed Indian, thick and hard as oak, and usually taciturn. He had been known to go for days at a time without ever more than grunting. But he was not a surly man, the way many taciturn individuals were. He was just not fond of talking.

The liveryman himself brought out Ladd's animal and rigged it in silence. When he handed over the reins, he still said nothing, but he winked as he walked away.

They did not head northward up through town. Simon Terry, the blacksmith, led out, and Simon did not like ostentation of any kind, so he led them up the back alley out

77

of town. That way they would not be viewed by the townsfolk as grim and relentless upholders of the law, which, although they might be, Simon did not like to have folks say about them. Also, if they came slinking back perhaps in the night having failed at their undertaking, it would be a lot easier to live with the failure if they hadn't pretended to be mighty manhunters on their way out of town.

As far as Ladd Buckner was concerned, he wasn't involved in any of this; he was only interested in studying the distant countryside and the even more distant mountain slopes, and trying to imagine where exactly those surviving outlaws had gone. The only thing he was certain of, as they angled back around and got atop the stage road northward beyond town, was that there had been only three survivors who had fled out of Piñon with their canvas sack full of bank money.

VIII

Because it was a moonless night with plenty of watery star shine, it was inevitable one of them would comment upon the visibility. Joe Reilly said: "I remember back during the war going out on a special patrol one night like this." Maybe Joe had not meant to say more but the others waited and finally Joe finished it. "There was a bunch of Rebels in a spit of trees and they chased us two-thirds of the way back to our lines, shooting and hollering their darned heads off." Joe smiled in the gloom. "I was never so afraid in my life."

Dr. Orcutt smiled but neither the blacksmith nor the harness maker showed appreciation of Joe Reilly's little tale.

"In the dark can't no one see you very far ahead," stated the blacksmith, and kept on leading the way up the road in the direction the outlaws had gone.

"Yeah," said Ladd dryly, "and we can't see very far ahead, either, Mister Terry. If those men turned off left or right, we'll still be riding north come sunup."

The blacksmith turned his bearded countenance to gaze darkly at the speaker before saying: "They didn't turn off left or right, Mister Buckner."

That was all he said; he did not explain how he knew they had not turned off, nor even whether he actually knew this or was simply guessing about it. But Dr. Orcutt offered an explanation. "A stage driver coming south only a couple of hours after the robbery saw three hard-riding men, one with a canvas sack slung over his shoulder, going northward up into the pass through the yonder hills."

That was no certainty, but Ladd settled for it, and, if it turned out to be a fact that those had been the surviving outlaws, why then the posse men from Piñon were indeed on the right track and were also unlikely to be seen. Something had to be right; everything that had been done since the robbery and the killings could not have been wrong.

Simon and Joe Reilly knew the onward countryside the best, but Simon did not elaborate upon what lay ahead. Joe did. The nearest town was at the foot of the yonder hills upon the far side. Otherwise, there was nothing but cow country on both sides of the mountains, and the actual mountains themselves were of little value except for hunting and sometimes, at the higher elevations, also for fishing. Unless one considered their value as a hide-out. Joe Reilly recounted a tale of two fugitive renegades who had existed in the mountains by simply changing camps every four days, for three years, and even then, he said, they probably would not have been taken except that one of them developed appendicitis and his partner brought him out. The ill man died anyway, and his partner had been tried and sent to prison. Joe concluded this recitation with his own homily: "Since a man never knows what might happen to him, I guess the best thing is not to get into trouble with the law, eh?" No one answered.

The night turned chilly as they entered the distant foothills and began a steady ascent. It got colder each hundred yards or so they climbed toward the gunsight notch that served as the route from south to north, and from northward to southward in the direction of Piñon. Enos Orcutt dropped back to ride beside the fourth posse man, and to offer a cigar that Ladd refused in favor of a rolled cigarette of his own manu-facture. With looped reins and a turned-up collar, he said: "Doctor, what do they have in this town we're coming to directly? Boarding house, saloon, place for folks to put up tired horses?"

"All those things," agreed the doctor. "And a town constable named Brennan who is . . . well, so I've heard anyway . . . pur-chasable."

Ladd lit up and exhaled smoke. "Purchas-able?"

"If you were three outlaws with nine thousand dollars in a sack and needed some rest and a place to put up your horses for a while, maybe for five or six hours, you could

81

offer him a handful of greenbacks and he'd see to it that you got those things."

Ladd's gaze was saturnine. "Sure takes you a long while to say something, don't it?"

Dr. Orcutt's teeth shone in the silvery night. "I suppose it does." He continued to grin. "Let you in on another of my secrets, Ladd. I'm probably the worst marksman in the entire Arizona Territory."

"In that case, I'd appreciate it, Doctor, if you'd stay in front of me," said the harness maker, and grinned back for the first time since seeing that letter Enos Orcutt had brought down to the harness shop with him.

Ladd glanced up ahead a few yards where silent Simon Terry was slouching along beside loquacious and burly Joe Reilly. He was slightly amused. If there were ever opposites on the trail, it had to be those two. Orcutt, guessing Ladd's thought, sighed and softly spoke: "Different as they are, we couldn't be riding on a mission of this kind in better company."

There was an opportunity to ask for an elaboration of this statement but a distraction arrived in the form of a very large cougar whose tail alone was as long as most other cougars were in the body. All four horses reacted to the powerful scent of that killer cat in the same way, by shying violently and keeping their riders very busy for a number of uncertain moments, or until the astonished and frightened big cat had fled westerly across the road to disappear silently into the darkness without looking back.

Later, as they pushed steadily upward toward the top out of the pass, and the cold became more noticeable than ever, Joe Reilly produced a bottle of malt whiskey that he magnanimously passed around. It helped a little to keep chilled bodies warm.

Ladd considered asking how much farther they had to go before getting down upon the far side of the pass, but in the end said nothing for the fundamental reason that knowing how many additional miles he had yet to traverse was not going to minimize them, and, whether there were a lot more of them, or a lot less, he was still going to keep riding along until they had been covered. On this kind of a ride, about the only thing that truly mattered was that the men did not stop any more often than they had to, and that they steadily and doggedly persevered, which they did, and were still doing when the cold, hushed, and rather dismal world through which they were passing in wraith-like silence began to pale out a little at a time until visibility improved enough for them to be able to look back and see the uneven, spiky rims behind them, and to look outward and downward and see a partially fog-shrouded immense valley and prairie ahead of them. They could not see the town at all but it was down there. As Joe Reilly said: "The folks that built Paso, the town we're coming to, had their reasons for not advertising that they had a settlement out here. Back in those days these hills were alive with crawling bands of ragheads."

"They still are," grumbled the blacksmith, and as usual did not elaborate after making his statement.

Eventually, as the daylight began to strengthen even though there would be no sunrise for another hour or two, it became possible for the men dwarfed to ant size upon the high slope winding their way downward to see roof tops and uneven roads and several sets of more distant ruts heading toward the clutch of buildings, mostly made of logs, lying at the very base of the pass on the westerly side where the land was more open and amenable to settlement and to the kind of labor that went with creating a town, such as garden patches, little postage-stamp-size milk cow enclosures, and horse corrals. Paso, for all its relative age in this raw, new world, had not grown as had Piñon. Of course there was a reason for this, but to Ladd Buckner the reason was anything but obvious. In some ways he could see that Paso had advantages that Piñon did not possess. For example, Paso was sheltered in the lee of the mountains behind it from winter's worst storms. Also, since it was shaded by those same peaks and slopes, it would be much cooler in summertime, which was always a major consideration in Arizona Territory.

Then Simon Terry made a short remark and Ladd was enlightened a little on this topic. The blacksmith said: "Never had enough water down there. Dig wells all the time and never get more than a trough full a day out of each well."

All the other blandishments in the world would not make up for that kind of a fault. Ladd rode along alternately watching the town shape up below him, and also watching for the sun to appear over in the hazy-blurred east. They were cold and beard-stubbled from being in the saddle all night. They were also rumpled and somewhat red-eyed and doggedly bleak and rugged in their general appearance. If someone saw them riding along like this, at such an ungodly hour armed to the teeth and scarcely more than grunting back and forth as they came down closer to the rear of the town at the foot of the pass, it would be almost impossible to consider them as anything other than renegades of the same variety as the men they were pursuing.

Dr. Orcutt alone could make some claim to respectability because of his frock coat and his curly-brimmed derby hat, but as they progressed these adjuncts of a civilized existence became less and less respectable in appearance, and by the time they were coming down across the last mile or so toward Paso, down where the trail flattened out for an agreeable change, Dr. Orcutt more nearly resembled a raffish, sly, and conniving gambler, or perhaps a peddler of paste diamonds or water-divining rods, than a genuine physician and surgeon.

Ladd Buckner looked at his companions when the light got better and decided to himself that if the people of Paso had any reason to be suspicious of strangers, he and his associates were going to become targets of some hard and probably hostile looks. It also troubled him a little that the lawman of Paso might be a badge-toting renegade. After all, the men from Piñon were shortly going to be entering this individual's bailiwick only four in number, seeking three proven murderers and bandits, and, if the town marshal chose to resent the interference of the men from Piñon. . . .

Joe Reilly straightened a little in the saddle and called their attention ahead down the roadway where a stagecoach had just wheeled clear of the Paso station to head up into the pass. "Morning coach bound for Piñon," he said. The way he made that announcement set his companions to eyeing the oncoming vehicle as though it might be their last best opportunity to send back word to Piñon of their whereabouts.

Then Ladd put their position into perspective by saying: "You string out across the road to stop this stage, gents, looking as mean and dirty and gun handy as we look in this lousy gray light, and that gun guard up there is going to start shooting as sure as I'm a foot tall. We look more like highwaymen than posse men."

The stage came on, without slackening pace, and both the men upon the high seat reached for weapons that they balanced across their laps. They had indeed seen the four horsemen from Piñon and had indeed turned very wary of their presence upon the road so early in the day, armed as they were. Then the stage swept past without anyone on either side waving, which was customary, and Dr. Orcutt twisted to look after the coach as his horse headed back for the center of the road again in the thin dawn dust. Dr. Orcutt had never been stared at in quite that way before. It was both a revelation to him, and a distinct discomfort.

Finally they came down behind the town and smelled breakfast fires in the making, which reminded them that they as well as their horses had been without food for a very long while. All night long in fact. Nor did it help arrest this realization that, as they passed down through several crooked little back byways, they could distinctly smell meat and potatoes frying and coffee boiling.

Paso was still only partially stirring when they walked their horses into the yard of the combination horse trader and liveryman, dismounted wordlessly, and handed over their reins to the round-eyed night hawk who was about to go off duty. They said nothing to the night hawk, who was suddenly very wide-awake, and he said nothing to them. Up the road a man with an ample paunch stepped forth and hurled a dishpan of greasy wash-water out into the center of the roadway, then retreated back into his place of business, which had the legend *Café* emblazoned across one wavery glass window.

Simon Terry led off as usual, this time

making a beeline for that beanery. The sun still had not appeared over in the hazy east.

IX

The café man looked as askance at his odd assortment of very early diners as that worried night hawk had looked at the same crew out front of the Paso livery barn. But the café man was older, more scarred and worldly, and therefore less likely to open his mouth either in front of those four men, or behind their backs. He differed again from the night hawk; as soon as the liveryman showed up along with his day man, the night hawk fled up in the direction of the constable's office in the ugly little functional log building up at the extreme north end of town. Otherwise, Paso did not notice or record the arrival in town of a massively powerful dark, fully-bearded individual whose silent lips were almost completely hidden by his black beard, or his companion upon the café man's bench who was wearing a shoved-back little gray derby hat that at one time had been an epitome of frontier elegance but that now had a dent in front where it had connected with a low tree limb in the dark of the previous night, and another dent in the back where it had struck the road after falling from Enos Orcutt's head when the tree limb had made its connection.

The other two, Joe Reilly and Ladd Buckner, also differed. In fact there was almost nothing those four men seemed to have in common as they sat in strong silence, eating like wolves, except that each one of them was heavily armed and each one of them had evidently been in the saddle all night. The café man concentrated upon filling them up and keeping the coffee coming. He did not open his mouth unless he was spoken to, and he did not stare. He, too, had at one time many years ago arrived in Paso like this, except that he had come down from the north and the posse men who had hunted high and low for him had been told a deliberate lie by a Mexican shepherd, and had ridden off to the east into the mountains on a wild-goose chase. That had been twenty-one years ago, and unless they had finally given up the pursuit in disgust to return homeward, by now they probably were walking their horses across the underside of the earth somewhere, but, wherever they were, the café man had done well in Paso and proposed to continue to do well in Paso — by seeing nothing, knowing nothing, and above all else by saying nothing. Even when Joe Reilly asked about the town constable the only retort he got was when the café man leaned down, peered over Reilly's head out his fly-specked roadway window, then grunted and pointed in the direction of a burly, graying man strolling along upon the opposite plank walk in the direction of his log jailhouse.

"That's him," announced the café man. "Constable Lewis Brennan." Then the café man became very busy gathering up empty plates and cups.

The men from Piñon went out front just as the first rays of sunlight appeared over in the distant west up along some night-shrouded high peaks, creating an effect of breathtakingly soft beauty. They saw only that daylight was coming as Ladd Buckner, who had been turning their situation over and over in his head, offered a suggestion: "Four of us beard this crooked constable, and it'll be like a bunch of ducks in a rain barrel if he decides to be troublesome. You three circulate around town, apart from each other so's it won't look so much like we're invadin' this place, and I'll go see the constable." He looked around as though anticipating an argument. None came, so he finished it: "I'll walk down the roadway here, to the livery barn, out in plain sight when I've finished with the constable. You watch, and meet me down there for our next palaver." Again he looked around. "Someone know better?"

Even Joe Reilly shook his head. Ordinarily Joe would have had something to say. Already Joe had sought out and located the local saloon.

They split up. Two men watched this, the café man behind them in his place of business, who was very interested but who would never to his dying day say that he had seen anything out front this morning, and the weasel-faced little wispy livery barn night hawk, who would, on the opposite side of the same coin, never stop talking about this affair and his part in it as long as he lived.

Ladd rolled a cigarette upon the far side of the roadway and wagged his head a little. This situation was exactly like the one he had been involved with almost nine years ago in a place only slightly larger than Paso where he had been sent ahead by the outlaw crew he was riding with to reconnoiter the town. That time, all hell had busted loose, too. He lit up, blew smoke, and tried to guess what was going to happen in this place a half hour or so from now, for while there was no bank in Paso, and the town itself was still more drowsy than awake, cow country communities had an ability suddenly to awaken with guns in all the fists on both sides of a roadway in the twinkling of an eye.

He turned and paced up to the log jailhouse, opened the door, and nodded to the round-faced, lion-maned, coarse-featured man who looked up from behind a littered desk. " 'Morning, Constable," he said, and offered a little crooked smile.

The constable nodded, put aside the paper he'd been reading, and gestured toward a wired-together old chair. " 'Morning. Have a seat. Care for some coffee?"

Ladd had drunk his daily allotment over at the café and said so as he sat down, then he said: "I come north over the hills last night, Constable."

Constable Lewis Brennan had pale, stone-steady blue eyes and they did not leave Ladd's face. "Is that a fact?" he said in a tone of complete disinterest. "In the saddle all night, then?"

Ladd nodded. "All night. I and some friends were down at a place called Piñon. We . . . got sort of separated down there. My friends were coming up here to Paso. We talked a little about that before we got down there to Piñon."

Constable Brennan pursed his lips in a slight expression of impatience. "What's your name?" he asked.

"Smith. Just plain old Jack Smith."

"Well, plain old Jack Smith," commented the burly lawman, "if you got something particular to say, I wish to hell you'd say it, because I ain't had breakfast yet and I don't do very well on an empty gut."

"Three riders, Constable, coming down over those mountains in a kind of a hurry. Originally there were six of us."

Lewis Brennan's eyes began to mirror caution. "Three left? What happened over in Piñon?"

Ladd leaned to tramp his smoked-down cigarette into the rough floor planking and answered while he was still bending over with his face averted: "The whole god-damned town turned out to welcome us, Constable Brennan." Ladd jumped his eyes back to the lawman's face. "You curious about me knowing your name? My friends and I heard it a long ways from here. We heard that you kept a decent town at Paso, where folks in need of a little lay-over would be plumb safe."

Lewis Brennan's unwavering gaze showed the same shades of caution as he made a quiet long assessment of Ladd Buckner, and finally said: "Well, Mister Smith, every town's got places where men can sort of lay-over and be safe, and in every one of those towns I was ever in it was also sort of expensive to get that kind of privacy."

Ladd smiled without a shred of mirth. "Sure. Well, we got a canvas sack full of money down at the Piñon bank, Mister Brennan. My share is in that sack. You name your price and point me in the right direction, and I'll get the money for you."

Lewis Brennan sat a long while in total silence without so much as changing his facial expression, then, about when Ladd had almost decided Brennan might not speak again at all, he very quietly said: "Turn around, Jack Smith."

It was the tone not the words that conveyed the sense of deadly peril. Ladd straightened in the old chair, then slowly turned.

There was a small cell-room door over across the room, heavily reinforced with strap steel and massive round-headed big black bolts. Wood or not, it would have taken a cannon to have demolished that door, but it wasn't the door that held Ladd Buckner almost breathless; it was the trio of men standing over there, hatless and in their stocking feet as though they might have just been roused from a nap in the dingy cells behind them. Each man had a six-gun pointed squarely at Ladd Buckner.

Lewis Brennan said: "Gents, who is he?"

A venomous-looking man with perpetually squinted eyes and a bluish wound for a mouth said: "Damned if I know, Brennan. I never seen the bastard before. But you'd better disarm him, just in case he's one of them fellers that little runt from the livery barn was in here talking about a few minutes ago."

Brennan made no move to arise from behind his desk. "Disarm him yourself," he told the vicious-looking man, then sat there watching as another of those three men swore and walked over to yank away Ladd's holstered Colt.

At the same time this man, younger than the other two but just as deadly in the eyes, gently shoved Ladd's own gun barrel into his neck at the side, and slowly cocked it as he said: "Start explaining, mister, and you lie just once. . . ." He shoved the cold gun barrel harder into Ladd's neck muscles.

The third man in stocking feet suddenly said: "Hey, wait a minute. I know this feller. I saw him plenty of times up north. Give me a minute and his name'll come back."

The man with the cocked gun pressing

into flesh said — "He don't have no minute." — and shoved the gun again, making Ladd lean to get away from most of the pressure.

The older outlaw snarled. "Stop playing like you're some kind of lousy executioner and just be quiet for a minute." He stared steadily at Ladd, and finally cursed with feeling because he could not remember the name. "But god dammit, I know that face. That's him all right."

The first man to speak turned a little. "That's who?" he asked impatiently. "Where did you see him before?"

"At Canon City," said the older outlaw. "He was learning saddle and harness making the same as me, but he was in the bunch that went over in the afternoon. I seen him dozens of times when we passed on the way. . . . God dammit, Buckner! That's it. His name is Buckner and he was in for robbing stages."

"Banks," said Ladd, holding his head to one side. "Not stages, banks."

The younger man eased off with his pistol barrel a little and looked for instruction to the other older man in the cell-room doorway. That individual put up his Colt and folded his arms while he steadily stared at Ladd.

"Why?" he eventually said, "did you come in here and try that cock-and-bull story on Lew Brennan?"

Ladd risked raising a hand to shove the gun barrel still farther from his neck. The venomous-eyed young outlaw allowed his weapon to be pushed gently away. He in fact even stepped back a little, then passed around toward the corner of Lew Brennan's desk to hoist himself up a little and perch there.

Ladd improvised but he did not overplay it. "I was in the Piñon saloon when you hit that damned bank down there. I saw what happened, and, as soon as I could decently get shed of that town, I tried to catch up to you."

"Wait a minute," interrupted the Paso lawman. "Who else come up with you?"

Ladd scowled. "No one. I met some fellers striking their camp back up the mountains a few miles just ahead of daybreak, had some coffee with them, and rode on down with them. They're freighters on their way up to Denver. At least that's what they said, and I can tell you for a fact they sure as hell aren't range men. One of them even wears a derby hat."

"Never mind that crap," growled the outlaw with the folded arms over in the cell-room doorway. "Why did you try to catch up to us?"

Ladd let his gaze waver slightly. "You got a sack full of money down there in Piñon," he said. "I heard the barman down there telling folks you got nine thousand dollars."

Lew Brennan's pale eyes suddenly jumped from Ladd to the outlaw over in the doorway. The outlaw reddened slightly, then shrugged. "All right, we got nine thousand, Lew."

"You told me four thousand," snarled the lawman. "You louse, you gave me ten percent of four thousand."

"You'll get the rest of it directly," soothed the red-faced outlaw, and looked unhappily at Ladd Buckner. "Damn you anyway. What did you figure to do . . . catch us in our blankets last night and cut our throats and take the sack of money?"

"No," replied Ladd. "I was going to offer to guide you into the westerly mountains where no posse or no one else could find you. For a fee, of course."

X

The youngest of those three outlaws who was still sitting upon the edge of Brennan's desk appeared to have a change of attitude.

Earlier, he had seemed perfectly willing to blow Ladd Buckner's head off with Ladd's own gun; now, as he listened and looked, he appeared to be favorably impressed with Ladd's offer to help the outlaws escape.

"There's a hell of a lot of mountains in back of this place," he told the pair of older outlaws across the room. "We'd be foolish to try and keep to the damned roadway."

The bleak-eyed man who was in age between the youngest outlaw and the older one snarled his reply: "Yeah, and you'd take this feller at face value and tomorrow morning you'd be dead as hell out there somewhere, and cleaned out down to your socks."

The oldest outlaw ignored both his companions, as though this kind of bickering was routine between them. He said: "Hey, Buckner, you remember a feller named Reston up there in Canon City? Whatever become of him? We was. . . ."

"For Christ's sake," snarled the leader of these men, the outlaw who was still standing over there in the cell-room doorway with both arms folded across his chest, "don't either one of you have a lick of sense? Brennan, we got to find out about those freighters he come down here with."

The constable nodded. "That'll be easy enough. They're likely still around and their horses are down at the livery barn. I'll go look around a little." Brennan swung his attention back to Ladd Buckner. "You got guts," he said, sounding neither hostile nor commendatory. "If you lied, Jack Smith or whatever your name is, you're as good as dead."

Ladd, with enough time to formulate a defensive idea, said: "Constable, I can identify their outfits for you, and lead you up to them. They won't suspect anything coming from me."

Brennan was on his feet as he replied: "If they're just freighters passing through, why should they expect anything? And the livery-man can identify their outfits." He turned toward the cell-room doorway. "I get the feelin' our visitor here wants to get out of here."

"He'll be here when you get back," said the outlaw leader. "Dead or alive, he'll be here."

Ladd watched Constable Brennan leave the jailhouse with misgivings. Brennan would examine the horses, saddles, and effects of his companions from Piñon, and he would also make enquiries around town. Since Orcutt, Reilly, and Simon Terry would be expecting nothing, Brennan would also be able to walk up behind them more than likely. There was no way for Brennan not to return to the jailhouse with a report substantiating his suspicions, unless a miracle occurred, and Ladd Buckner had no faith in miracles.

He rolled a cigarette to occupy his hands, and, when the oldest outlaw filled in the unpleasant silence with another enquiry concerning a man they had both known in prison, Ladd was willing to tell what he knew. He and the oldest outlaw got into quite a conversation. The youngest outlaw listened, then leathered his Colt and yawned, walked around behind Brennan's desk, and sat down back there. The outlaw leader, though, was not nearly as impressed with Buckner's bona-fide outlaw credentials from Canon City. He was evidently one of those lifelong skeptics one encountered more, perhaps, among outlaws than among other kinds of people. He broke into the conversation between his older companion and Ladd Buckner by asking who else had taken the outlaw trail from Piñon.

Ladd told the truth. "As far as I know, there wasn't any pursuit."

The outlaw leader scoffed. "No pursuit? After we busted their bank and shot their citizens?"

"Maybe that's why," stated Ladd. "I can

tell you for a fact the whole darned town was stumbling over itself. And you killed their lawman, the only feller around who could organize and lead a posse."

The youngest outlaw smiled for the first time, but not at Ladd, at his leader. "I told you Henry'd fix it for us."

Their leader ignored that statement to say: "By now, though, they sure as hell got a posse on the way."

Ladd was cautious when he answered that. "I'd guess by now they have, but if you follow me off into these mountains back yonder, all the posses on earth can't find you. Mister, I can set you up a camp in a big meadow back in there where the ragheads hid out for ten years without anyone ever finding them."

"Yeah? And suppose they're still in those mountains," stated the head outlaw. "Not too long ago some cattle outfit over around Piñon got hit by a bushwhacking band of 'em."

Ladd brushed this aside. "Weren't more than eight in that bunch. Reservation jumpers, I'd guess. Anyway, I can take you back in there where even the ragheads can't find you. I can set you up alongside a lake in there that's got trout in it as thick as your arm, and all you'll have to do is lie around, fish a little, and get fat, safe as you can be."

There was nothing wrong with the presentation or with the idea; if there was one thing renegades of this kind yearned for, it was a place where they could stop running and hiding, and sleeping with a cocked gun at their side. Ladd knew the psychology of men like these, which was why he had fabricated this alluring prospect. But that man over in the cell-room doorway was not as influenced as were his companions. He said: "Buckner, a feller who would try what you tried by coming after us like a lousy coyote skulking along would work for the law."

Ladd flared up. "What law? Damn it all, you saw him get killed back there."

"Not him," snapped the outlaw. "The law that pays bounties for us fellers."

The oldest outlaw broke in: "Cass, what in the hell . . . ? Listen to me. Let Buckner guide us back into them mountains where we can hide out for a month or two. If he turns out to be double-crossing us some way, we'll simply kill him."

"Sure," assented their leader in a voice heavy with sarcasm, "we'll kill him . . . after he maybe leads us up in front of a lousy posse. Walt, just keep out of this, will you?" The spokesman faced Ladd again. "I wouldn't trust you as far as I could throw you," he stated. "As far as I'm concerned, it'll be up to Brennan what he wants to do with you. You come in here lyin' in your teeth as neat as a whistle. Not only that, but you had to go and say we got nine thousand instead of the four thousand Brennan figured we'd got."

"How the hell was I to know you'd lied to him?" demanded Ladd. "And you don't have to trust me. All you've got to do is keep me in front of you until we're so far back in those mountains the Indians couldn't even find us. Mister, why would I be willing to go back in there with you fellers if I didn't know exactly where to hide you? I didn't come down in the last rain. I know you can shoot me if I don't deliver what I say I'll deliver. Your trouble is, damn it all, you got your tail feathers burned off down at Piñon and now you figure everyone is against you."

The youngest outlaw chimed in with an opinion of his own. "We got our tail feathers singed all right. That lousy town accounted for damned good men. But by God I paid 'em back. I shot their banker and his dog robber, that other feller behind the wicket in their bank. I evened things up a little."

Cass remained over in the doorway, arms

crossed, waiting for the younger man to say all he had to say, then the leader of these men asked Ladd a question: "Who was that son-of-a-bitch come out of the jailhouse and cut loose on us out front of the bank?"

Ladd lied as deftly as he'd been lying for the past fifteen minutes. "Feller by the name of Sanders. All I know about him is what I heard in the saloon. He was down there near the harness works when the marshal walked out. Someone said Sanders is a former lawman from down in Texas. That's all I heard."

"We owe him," said Cass gruffly.

Ladd shrugged that off. "All right. But you sure as hell hadn't better try going back over there to settle up with him. Not for a couple of months anyway." Ladd scratched his middle and glanced toward the door. He had been bold up to this point and he might just as well continue being bold, because when Constable Lewis Brennan walked through that doorway again, Ladd Buckner's chances for survival were going to start plummeting immediately.

"Too bad Henry couldn't signal about this Sanders feller, too," said the youngest renegade from his comfortable position in the constable's chair.

That touched a nerve in Cass. "Damn it!"

the outlaw leader exclaimed. "Why couldn't he have come up north of town and warned us about that feller, instead of just staying in the lousy store and signaling where the town marshal was?"

The way the youngest renegade sprang to the defense of Henry, whoever he was, seemed to imply at least a friendship. "You yourself told me all he had to do was put on one of those four hats in the store-window so's we'd know where the marshal was. And he done it, Cass, exactly like you said. You can't blame Henry for what happened."

Walt, the oldest outlaw, went to the stove, padding soundlessly across the floor in his stocking feet, and hefted the coffee pot over there atop the wood stove. Evidently Walt's hard existence had inured him to cold stale coffee, because he poured himself a cup of the stuff and went over to a wall bench to sit and sip. He seemed very relaxed now, very comfortable in fact, and the fact that he and his friends were inside a jailhouse evidently did not trouble Walt in the least. At least this particular jailhouse belonged to them as a hide-out, and perhaps that amused Walt. Ladd had heard a lot of outlaws up in Canon City boast of bribing lawmen. They always seemed to derive enormous satisfaction from their ability to do it. Maybe Walt got the same satisfaction from having the run of a jailhouse whose legal custodian had been bought with some of the blood money from Piñon.

Cass straightened up over in the doorway and walked to a front wall window to stoop slightly and peer out. "What's keeping Brennan?" he growled.

Walt idly said: "Maybe he's the feller we'd ought to worry about instead of Buckner."

Cass turned. "You damned fool," he growled, and went to work rolling a cigarette, scowling unhappily as he did it.

Ladd tried to guess what Cass's weakness was and decided it had to be his inherent mistrust of everyone. But how something like that could be exploited eluded Ladd. Gradually it began also to occur to him that Brennan had been out there an inordinate length of time. The possibilities were tantalizing, and they were also manifold, but Ladd's main consideration was what would happen if Brennan returned, and he thought he had a fair idea about that.

Cass blew smoke at the ceiling, then stepped back to lean and peer out into the roadway again. Paso was quiet, as it probably was two-thirds of the time. A morning stage arrived from across the vast expanse of prairie land northward, and momentarily this appeared to rouse the place a little. A man's hearty laughter up the road beyond sight rang reassuringly.

Walt said: "Brennan better get his butt back here. He's got to fetch us some breakfast yet this morning."

Ladd, remembering what the lawman had told him a half hour earlier, offered a placating suggestion: "He's probably at the café filling up. He said he hadn't eaten."

Cass sighed, and padded back over into the cell-room doorway to finish his smoke and be thoughtful. He ignored Ladd. It was very probable that he had already made up his mind what to do about Ladd Buckner. If this were so, and considering Cass's suspicious, deadly nature, it was not difficult to imagine what his decision amounted to.

That coach that had rattled into town raised a fine dust part way along the central thoroughfare. Ladd did not leave his chair but he could see the dust in the air. He was frankly fearful and he had every right to be that way. Even though Reilly, Terry, and Orcutt would be wary and watchful, they would be susceptible to Brennan's approach; not knowing what had happened inside the jailhouse or what lies Ladd had told, they would be unable to offer believable support for those lies — and that would simply mean that, when Brennan walked through the door of the jailhouse, Ladd Buckner would be living on borrowed time. He had no illusions, either, about Walt, the moderately congenial old renegade who had recognized Ladd from their prison days. Walt, Cass, and especially that venomous-eyed youngest outlaw would gun down Ladd Buckner without a qualm. Inside the Paso township jailhouse, they would not dare use guns, so they would use knives or clubs, whatever came handy, but they would kill Ladd Buckner as surely as the sun would set this evening.

XI

Brennan did not return and Cass was more worried than he allowed the others to see. How Ladd knew this was so was in part a deduction based upon the outlaw leader's increasingly waspish and derogatory comments to his partners, and also by the way Cass paced the room from time to time, always ending up over along the front wall where he leaned down to look out of a barred jailhouse window.

Ladd worried, also, but in a different way.

In fact, the longer Brennan remained away, the better Ladd's chances seemed to be. At least they seemed to be better in the area of personal survival. Until Lew Brennan returned and blew Ladd Buckner's story sky high with the simple truth, no one was going to attempt to murder Ladd. Cass no doubt would murder him offhandedly, but now neither Walt nor the youngest renegade was still that deadly minded. Particularly old Walt, who talked to Ladd about the old days up at Canon City as though they were alumni from the same school. Maybe, in a sense, this was a logical spirit since Walt had obviously never attended much school.

Finally someone out front stamping up off the roadway to cross planking in the direction of the jailhouse door brought the three hiding men to their feet. Walt and the youngest outlaw hastened over to be near the cell-room door. All three of them sidled through and Cass reached with one hand, partially to close the door. He shot a savage glare at Ladd and wigwagged with a drawn pistol. Ladd had no difficulty in understanding, even though Cass did not say a word.

The man who entered the jailhouse was not Constable Brennan. He was heavy-set, bald, and slovenly, and he stared at Ladd Buckner as though he had expected to see someone besides a total stranger sitting there. He said: "Howdy, where's Lew Brennan this morning?"

Ladd offered a bland reply. "I reckon he's around somewhere. I haven't seen him in the past half hour or more."

The heavy-set man stroked his chin and continued to gaze at Ladd. "You a friend of Lew's?" he asked, and Ladd smiled a little.

"You might say that," he conceded. "Thing is, you'd be askin' the wrong feller, wouldn't you? Only Lew Brennan could say whether he considers me his friend or not."

The heavy-set man looked a little disgusted with that answer. He glanced toward the desk, around the room, then turned back to place a hand upon the door latch as he said: "Tell him Johnny Wheeler was in and I'll be up at the stage station for another half hour or so, if he wants to look me up." Johnny Wheeler swung back the door.

"Anything else you want me to tell him?" asked Ladd.

Wheeler considered a moment before saying: "I reckon you can tell him I picked up some word on them fellers who shot up Piñon and robbed the bank down there. Tell him I got some information on them boys up at Pine Grove. The law up there went and captured one of them fellers. Well, he

112

can look me up." Wheeler bobbed his head and departed.

Ladd arose, stepped to the door, dropped the bar into place across the back of the door, then turned as Cass and his companions came back into the office from the cell-room corridor.

"Who in the hell," mused Walt, "could some cow town constable have arrested for what we done down in Piñon, I wonder?"

Cass was also interested. In a different tone of voice than he'd used toward Ladd up to now, he said: "You plumb certain those three fellers we had to leave down in Piñon are dead?"

Ladd knew for a fact that each of those men lay dead in Enos Orcutt's shed, but to help his own situation a little by creating more diversion, he said: "That's what they told me in the saloon. They said that Sanders feller dropped all three of them and they was dead." Ladd shrugged heavy shoulders. "But I didn't see their corpses. All I know is what they were saying around the saloon."

Cass turned to the youngest outlaw. "Abner, you was out there in front after we came from the bank. Did you see 'em lying out in the roadway?"

Abner nodded. "I seen them, Cass, blood

113

all over them and the ground. But, like Buckner says, maybe. . . ." Abner looked at Ladd for support and did not finish his remark.

Ladd frowned a little. "Why would one of them go north to the next town instead of looking you fellers up here in Paso?"

It was a valid question. Walt echoed it to Cass. "That's not very sensible. They knew we'd paid up in advance to hide out in this damned jailhouse until the noise died down. Cass, why would one of them head on northward and by-pass us here in Paso?"

Before the leader could reply, Ladd said: "Because it's not one of your crew, Walt. It's some other feller up in Pine Grove that the law leaned down on. Maybe it's the law who made up that story so's he could maybe collect bounty on someone. Maybe it was the feller he leaned on acting like he was a lot bigger than he is."

—Cass nodded. "That's got to be it. Something like that." He returned to the front window again and stooped down. As he systematically studied as much of the main roadway as could be seen, he said: "That son-of-a-bitch Brennan." He added nothing to this, and a moment later, when he started to turn away, he froze at the window for a moment, then swore exasperatedly. "Two

114

men coming across from the store. Let's get out of sight." He turned, looked at Ladd, and made a small hand gesture. "Get rid of them," he ordered, and retreated with Walt and Abner beyond the cell-room door again.

This time when the visitors walked in Ladd arose and went to stand over near the gun rack on the far wall, his right side turned away from the pair of cowmen who looked from the desk on around the room and over to Ladd as one of them gruffly said: "Where's Brennan? We got business with him."

Ladd answered forthrightly. "He was here about an hour ago. Since then he hasn't been back. If you've got a message, I'll be glad to give it to him for you."

"There are Apaches on the east range," said the gruff-voiced older man, his expression reflecting the bleak mood he was in. "This here is Jim Morgan. I'm Jeff Longstreet. You see Brennan, you tell him we come by to see if he wants to do anything, and, if he don't, we'll do it for him. We'll make up some riding posses and chase those darned redskins all the way down to the border and across it. You hear?"

Ladd could have heard the angry cowman if he'd been out back in the alley. "I'll tell him when he gets back, Mister Longstreet.

By the way, if you really want to recruit riders to go against the Indians, just post a notice that you're paying a decent wage and you'll get all the men you'll need."

Old Longstreet grunted. "I don't need advice, young feller, and us fellers who run cattle on the east range don't need recruits. We got a small army of riders betwixt the lot of us."

Longstreet and his silent companion stamped out of the office. From the cell-room doorway Cass said: "Buckner, I thought you said there weren't no Apaches in the hills around here?"

Ladd did not recall having said any such thing. But he did remember saying he could hide the outlaws so well in the mountains even the Indians could not find them. He repeated this, then he also said: "No better way under the sun to get out of this country, if you want to leave it, than to join a raghead-hunting expedition, and just keep on going. Posse men don't go traipsing after outlaws over territory inhabited by hostiles."

Cass stared. "You're about as smart as Walt!" he exclaimed. "And what would the ragheads do if they seen the three of us out there alone, crossing their damned territory? I'll tell you what they'd do. . . . ." But Cass did not have a chance to finish his state-

116

ment. Out front a man swung his horse toward the jailhouse and stepped from the saddle with a loud grunt, and Cass reached again to pull the cell-room door almost closed.

This time, when the stranger walked in, he brought a scent of sage and heat and open spaces with him. He was, like the pair of older men who had previously visited the jailhouse, a range cattleman. His attire spoke volumes about his ability, his rugged confidence, and his cow savvy. He was tall and squinty-eyed and pleasant in the face, although his hide was leathery, lined, and currently unshaved. He smiled pleasantly at Ladd and asked about Brennan. When Ladd said the lawman wasn't around this tall, rugged individual shoved back his hat, fished forth his tobacco sack and brown cigarette papers, and went to work as he laconically said: "My name is Harrison. Brennan will know me if you tell him that name." Harrison lit his smoke and continued to study Ladd Buckner. "I got raided last night and lost maybe thirty, forty steers and heifers on the east range."

Ladd said: "Ragheads. Do you know a feller named Longstreet?"

"We got adjoinin' ranges," said Harrison. "Him, too?"

"Yes. He and a man named Morgan were in here not more than minutes ago. The Apaches hit them, too."

Harrison smoked and gazed at Ladd, then gazed around the office, and for a man who had lost cattle to Indians he did not act nearly as fired-up as Longstreet had acted. "When will Lew be back?" he asked.

Ladd answered cautiously: "I don't know, but he shouldn't be much longer. I think he just went around town somewhere."

"You a friend of his?"

Ladd shrugged. "We know each other."

Harrison did not appear to be in any hurry to leave. Unlike the other visitors who had stopped by this morning, Harrison acted more as though he were paying a social call than as though he were an outraged cowman. In fact he strolled toward a chair and with one hand on the back of it, he said: "If it won't be too long, I could set here and wait."

Ladd had mixed feelings about this. He needed reinforcements but there was no guarantee Harrison would turn out to be his ally in the event of trouble. On the other hand, as long as the range cattleman was there, in the office, even if Brennan walked in, he could hardly afford to denounce Ladd in front of his friend. Ladd decided not to protest, and asked if Harrison wanted some cold, stale coffee. The cowman surprised Ladd. "That's a right good idea," he said, and pulled aside the chair as he sat down facing the side wall and the back wall of the jailhouse office. He seemed never to allow his eyes to widen out of their perpetual squint, nor did it help that cigarette smoke trickled upward, also compelling him to keep his eyes narrowed.

Ladd drew off a mug of the bitter coffee and handed it across. Harrison accepted it gravely. "Much obliged," he said, and shoved out long legs that he crossed at the ankles as he studied Ladd some more. "Seems to me I may have seen you around the countryside somewhere, friend. I run cattle on the north and east ranges." He smiled a trifle. "I also got 'em on the south and west ranges, only they aren't supposed to be in them places."

Harrison rambled on. He was a pleasant man to talk to as Ladd discovered while they faced one another across the room, and it also developed that Harrison was an observant individual. He said: "Mister, did you know you'd lost your six-gun?"

Ladd looked down. He had made a particular point of trying to keep his right side turned to the wall. Evidently he had not wholly succeeded. "Left it with a gunsmith to be fixed," he lied. "The firing pin is so badly chipped it only detonates the bullets about every third or fourth time."

Harrison smoked, sipped coffee, and offered no comment for a while, not until he leaned to drop his smoke and stamp on it. Then he said: "We don't have no gunsmith in Paso."

Ladd reddened a little. "Didn't leave it to be fixed in Paso, friend. I left it up at . . . Pine Grove . . . to be fixed."

Harrison raised skeptical eyes. "And since then you've been riding around wearing that empty holster? Well, *amigo,* we all got different ideas, don't we? Me, I got no use for guns at all. I wear one because I figure I'd get killed within a week or two if I didn't wear one, but guns are the devil's tools for a fact. Nothing good ever comes of men relying upon guns."

Ladd tried to figure this man out, and he could not even come close to doing it, and he knew he was not coming close.

XII

Cass eased the cell-room door open as quietly and as surreptitiously as he had done with Ladd Buckner, but this time the man

120

sitting before the constable's desk was facing in that direction and saw the three men with their aimed six-guns. Harrison did not lower the coffee cup but continued to sip coffee for a moment, for as long as it took him carefully to determine what was across the room from him. Then, gradually, he lowered the cup and blew a little smoke but neither moved nor opened his mouth. He seemed surprised, but he also seemed perfectly capable of living with this astonishing situation. He leaned to put the cup atop Brennan's desk, then he eased back again as Cass and Walt pushed out of the cell-room corridor, and youthful Abner briskly shouldered past the older men and approached Harrison with his cocked Colt pointed squarely at the cattleman's face.

Harrison turned slightly to cast a sardonic look in Ladd Buckner's direction. "Friends of yours?" he asked quietly.

Ladd did not answer; he simply stood and watched Abner disarm the range man exactly as Abner had also disarmed him. When Harrison was defanged, Walt lowered his gun a notch and said: "Cass, it's goin' to get a little crowded in here directly."

Cass was in no mood for levity and acted as though he had not heard the older man. He cocked his head though, as heavy footfalls approaching from the south out upon the plank walk made a solid, heavy sound. All of them listened, including Harrison. Ladd Buckner was half of the opinion that this time whoever that was out yonder would stride right on past. Cass did not feel this confident, apparently, because he snarled for his companions to retreat again, and led the way into the cell-room corridor. They had scarcely got the door almost closed before Lew Brennan walked in out of the hot sunlight of mid-morning.

Brennan stared from Ladd to Harrison, then over toward the cell-room doorway as Cass stepped forth with his gun hand stone steady and said: "Where in the hell have you been? What took you so long?"

Instead of replying at once to the outlaw's question Constable Brennan pointed: "What the hell are you doing with this feller? He's a local cowman."

Cass turned bitingly sarcastic again. "Yeah, we know he's a local cowman, and we also know that, if you had shagged your butt back here at a decent time, you could have handled the flow of callers been coming in here all morning to complain about some lousy Indians running off livestock on the east range. Instead, you been horsing around over at the saloon, or somewhere, and we didn't even get any breakfast. Brennan, I got half a notion to. . . ."

"Wait a minute," protested the law officer. "What was the sense of taking this one? He's harmless. He runs cattle west of town . . . and now you've gone and made a lousy mess of everything."

Brennan looked at the cowman and Harrison smoked, looked steadily back, and, when the silence began to draw out, he dryly said: "Lew, you always were a worthless bastard."

Normally, perhaps, Brennan would have hurled himself upon someone who had insulted him like that, but right at this moment Brennan's thoughts were upon a much more critical phase of what had happened in his absence. Harrison, the respectable local cowman, would be able to identify the Piñon bank robbers and killers as the same men Brennan was hiding in the Paso jailhouse. What Cass actually had done by taking Harrison captive was destroy Brennan's credibility in the town where Brennan was not just the local representative of the law, but where Brennan also lived and enjoyed living. Now, when the outlaws departed, Brennan would also have to depart. Unless something happened to Harrison. But Brennan did not think of that at this moment; he instead turned a brooding gaze on Cass and Walt and the youngest renegade, then jerked his head in Ladd's direction.

"There's just one of those freighters still in town. A big feller with a beard all over his face and he can't talk very well."

Ladd scarcely drew a breath. For Lew Brennan to identify Simon Terry as a freighter implied that Brennan had not as yet discovered the hoax. Ladd was almost ready to start breathing again.

Cass holstered his six-gun. "All right. So Buckner told us the truth about how he got here. That's the only true thing he told us. Now we got to get away from here."

Brennan frowned. "You don't go alone." He pointed. "You fixed it so's I can't stay the minute you let this range man figure things out."

Abner disagreed with this. "Shoot the son-of-a-bitch," he said. "Get away from his chair and I'll do it."

Cass swore. "You crazy devil, Abner. You ease off the hammer of that gun. You pull a trigger in here and, log walls or not, everyone in this lousy town'll hear the shooting and come a-running. Anyway, this cowman isn't our headache. I said ease down the hammer on that damned gun!"

Abner obeyed. He even leathered his Colt but his expression was sullen and he turned away from Cass to face in Buckner's direction.

"What a god-damn' mess," groaned the constable, moving around to his desk chair and sinking down over there.

Harrison dropped his smoke and stepped on it. He shot Ladd a glance, then swung slightly to rake the three renegades with another look. He sighed audibly and waggled his head as though he were monumentally disgusted. "And I thought I had trouble," he muttered, "when I come into town this morning. Lew . . . ?"

Brennan snapped at the cowman. "You do have trouble, Harrison." Brennan turned toward Cass. "Remember, I got money coming. Ten percent of nine thousand." Brennan leaned thick arms atop his desk. Evidently he was beginning to try and ameliorate his dilemma, and, since money was apparently his measure of all things and all kinds of success, he was beginning to reason that he would be paid well for having to flee the country.

Cass did not even answer that, did not even act as though he had heard it. "We'll set around here until nightfall, then we'll have to ride on." Cass said this for the benefit of Abner and old Walt, his fellow renegades, but to Ladd it had the unpleasant sound of something a cold-blooded individual might say whose private decision, whatever it was, had been reached. If this were so, then Ladd felt instinctively that he and perhaps the range cattleman were not going to see another sunrise. If the renegades abandoned Paso and their hide-out, which had become increasingly perilous for them this day, they were probably not going to leave a couple of hostages behind who could not only identify them but who could also recall a number of particular details regarding each renegade.

Walt said: "Take Buckner along and head back into the mountains."

Cass flared back. "You darned fool, haven't you heard what these cowmen been saying all day? There's Indians out there. If they could pick up the tracks of just four riders, they'd be after us like a pack of wolves after a crippled doe."

Walt was not affronted, perhaps because he was by this time well accustomed to being derided by Cass. He shrugged and said: "All right. Then where? We can't go south again. What does that leave?" Walt had a point. If they went northward or eastward, they ran a fine chance of encountering those rampaging Apaches. Southward lay the aroused area around Piñon. Westerly, as the range cattleman had been saying since his arrival at the jailhouse, there had also been an Apache raid. "Stay right where we are," said Walt, looking sardonically at the outlaw leader, "and take us some more hostages." He jerked his head in Brennan's direction. "It'll look like we got Lew here as a prisoner and that had ought to get him out of trouble with the folks here in his town."

"Lew?" exclaimed Cass. "Who gives a damn about Lew? We got just three hides to worry about, and that don't include Lew Brennan." Cass turned upon the constable. "How good is the road west of here along the foothills?"

Brennan didn't answer, the range cattleman did. "Lousy," he said. "In places it hasn't been filled in since the rains of last winter. You don't have trouble on horseback but you can't use it with wheels and teams."

Cass glared. "I didn't ask you!"

Harrison was uncowed. "I know that. But I happen to have ridden in by that road this morning and I don't know when was the last time Brennan was out that way." Harrison continued to look steadily at the glowering outlaw. "You might make it out of here on a stagecoach. So far the ragheads haven't attacked one of them, and, if you could keep 'em from downing the harness horses while you were protected inside the rig with plenty of ammunition, I think you could probably make it all the way up to Pine Grove. There hasn't been any redskin trouble up there yet. Not that I've heard of anyway."

Abner and Walt exchanged a glance, then turned to see what their leader's reaction to this might be. Cass did not keep them wondering very long. He sneered at Harrison. "What the hell do you take us for, anyway? If the ragheads are on the north range beyond Paso, they'd sight anything as big as a stagecoach from a couple of miles out. I think you're trying to get us killed. That's what I think."

Harrison still did not drop his eyes. "Mister, if you got a way out of Paso, and you don't get all the wood and what-not around you when you make your run for it . . . they'll bury you right here. Go ahead and try it on horseback."

Cass went to the window and leaned to gaze out into the sun-bright roadway. Paso lay utterly still on all sides. For a long while the outlaw chieftain looked out and around, then he very slowly straightened up and turned. "Brennan," he said sharply, "there's no one in the damned roadway. Even the tie racks are empty."

Paso's lawman heaved up to his feet and crossed over to look out. Cass was correct; the town was as silent and empty-seeming as a cemetery. Brennan looked more puzzled than anxious as he strained to see up the roadway as far as possible before saying: "It's high noon. This time of year it's pretty much always like this in the middle of the day . . . and later, too . . . for as long as the heat lasts."

But when Lewis Brennan turned back toward his desk, Ladd Buckner got the impression from his expression that Brennan was a lot less puzzled now, that he was just plain worried.

Cass was slightly less anxious after Brennan's pronouncement, but, when he, too, moved away from the window, he shot a cold look around at them all, then echoed the constable by saying: "What a damned mess. The whole blasted thing's got out of hand." He fixed Ladd Buckner with a vicious look. "When you walked in and commenced your lousy lying, the trouble started."

Ladd borrowed a leaf from the cattleman's book by saying: "The trouble started down in Piñon, not up here."

Cass ignored that contradiction to say: "What idea have you got about us pulling out of here?"

"I've been telling you all morning," replied Ladd, "to sneak out the back way when no one is looking and head up into the mountains with me. I don't see that you can do anything else, now that there's a band of raghead marauders on the upper cattle range. Like you said yourself, if you bust out of Paso heading across all that flat, open country, they'll see you sure as hell."

"Not in the dark," said Cass.

Harrison spoke up. "You can't get plumb across it by morning even if you ride fast all night. You'd still be sitting ducks out there."

Abner turned on his chieftain. "Damn it, Cass, quit buttin' your head against a stone wall. These fellers know this lousy country. You heard 'em. We can't get out of here except by Buckner's route."

Cass turned. "Sonny," he said in his most condescending tone, "all these fellers want is to see the three of us get killed. All I'm trying to do is to prevent that from happening. If you want to head out on your own, there is the damned door and good riddance."

Abner did not say any more. He and Walt looked a little more worried as time passed, but they did not again offer to challenge Cass's comments or his judgment.

XIII

Ladd longed to cross the room and look out into the roadway. He was confident that something had happened out there. Perhaps Orcutt, Terry, and Reilly had guessed his difficulty inside the jailhouse, and maybe they had somehow learned that the outlaws they had come north to find were also inside the jailhouse, but whatever people knew around Paso, it most probably had something to do with the men in the jailhouse. If he'd dared, he would have engaged Lewis Brennan in conversation to see if Brennan had even unconsciously seen or heard anything that might have had significance. Instead of doing any of these things Ladd remained over along the rear wall smoking and being unobtrusive. Of one thing he was reasonably certain — this charade was not going to last much longer. If the men outside didn't force the issue, the outlaws themselves would do so.

Cass in particular was becoming increasingly worried and restless as time passed. He walked to the stove to get some coffee and cast a sulphurous glance in Ladd Buckner's direction. "How could we get plumb clear of this town," he asked surlily, "and into those mountains without anyone knowing we'd done it, for as long as we'd need to get a good start?"

Ladd answered bluntly: "You said it yourself. Wait until nightfall, then leave in the dark."

The outlaw lifted his coffee cup. "We got to have horses," he said, "and not just old pelters, either. Riding the mountains requires good saddle stock."

Ladd agreed. "We'll need good stock, no question about it, but they've got it around Paso. Down at the livery barn, maybe, or in the sheds around town. We can take care of that, too, after dark when most folks'll be eating supper."

Walt smiled encouragingly. He had been favoring Ladd Buckner right from the start, and now, when it seemed that Cass was going to adopt Ladd's scheme for getting them out of their predicament, Walt not only felt vindicated, he was also showing by his broad smile that he felt that way.

Abner was sulking and he was bored. The prospect of dying in this mean little village did not appear to trouble him, probably because Abner, who was a totally depthless individual, never considered death as being applicable to him. Death only arrived to snuff out the life of others. And Abner was patently a person who required movement, change, action. Being cooped up in the log jailhouse of a place called Paso brought out his latent restlessness. He probably would have paced, if he'd thought of it or if his partners would have tolerated it. As it was, he leaned upon the wall looking mercilessly at the others and occasionally leaning down to look out of the window. It was one of the times that he was doing this, squinting into the sunshine out in the roadway, that he suddenly said: "There is something going on up at the saloon."

Cass walked over and so did Walt, but when the older outlaw would also have leaned to look out, with his back to the room, Cass growled at him, so Walt shrugged and turned fully to face the hostages.

After a moment of watching and looking, the outlaw leader straightened around, frowning in Brennan's direction. "Take a look," he commanded, "and tell me what it's all about."

The lawman walked over and swung slightly to one side in order to be able to see northward in the roadway. After a moment he stepped back, straightening up.

"Looks like one of the cow outfits just rode in . . . something like that."

Cass eyed the lawman. "Can you go up there and find out?"

Brennan said: "Sure, why couldn't I?"

"You was worried a while back about folks knowing you were hiding us in here."

Brennan jutted his jaw. "Harrison there would tell folks, if he got out of here . . . *when* he gets out of here. But right now they wouldn't know anything. At least I can't see how they'd know anything."

Cass nodded. "Go up and nose around, but be careful. It's too darned quiet out there, it seems to me. Pick up all the information you can."

Abner went over to hold the door open and to say: "Constable, ask about them damned Indians. Find out if they're likely to be into them mountains back there."

As Brennan stepped outside, he nodded his head as though he were agreeing with the youngest killer's interest in marauding broncos, but his eyes were moving swiftly left and right along the empty roadway, too, so perhaps his nodding was simply perfunctory.

Walt turned to Ladd Buckner with an expression of confidence. "We could take that son-of-a-bitch with us for a shield," he said. "I never could abide folks who wear badges, not even crooked ones."

Harrison glanced at Walt, then turned his attention back to Cass and Abner over along the front wall watching Brennan's progress on a diagonal course up the roadway. If Harrison was entertaining some notion of perhaps jumping Walt and trying to get Walt's weapon before Abner and Cass turned around, he had to abandon the idea. Cass abruptly turned to look at the others, then to sigh and walk around to ease down at the lawman's desk and lean back in quiet thought.

There was still a long time before nightfall. Like it or not, for all of them there were a number of long hours yet to be waited out. Cass addressed the cowman. He seemed to have developed a grudging respect for Harrison, perhaps because the cowman had not once been cowed by Cass's evil disposition or menacing attitude. "You figure we'd make it going off with Buckner into the mountains?" Cass asked, and the range cattleman shifted his attention to the outlaw leader but for a long while he seemed to be considering his reply. Eventually he said: "Yeah, I figure you could make it. I know I could . . . providin' I could safely get into the forest cover back there. It's a hell of a big chunk of territory."

"And as soon as we're gone, you'll tell everyone where we went," said Cass.

This time the range cowman smiled. "Sure, that'd be natural, wouldn't it? Trouble is, mister, without Brennan there's no law in Paso to recruit a posse, and, if folks hear that you're the same bunch who shot up Piñon and killed some people, I sort of doubt that anyone could get up a posse. Folks usually figure that, if something don't harm them, why then it's got to be someone else's problem, not theirs."

Cass said no more for a while. He did not seem convinced by Harrison's logic. After all, Cass had already used up two of his lives and only had one life left. Those were the circumstances that made cautious men of a great many outlaws. If things turned out as Harrison thought they might, that would be fine. If they didn't turn out that way. . . .

Abner, speaking from the front window, caught everyone's attention: "Brennan's coming back. Looks like no one suspected nothing when they was talkin' to him up there." Abner moved clear of the window and started to form a cigarette.

Ladd Buckner could feel his stomach tightening again exactly as it had when Brennan had returned to the jailhouse the first time. One thing Ladd suspected was that his friends from Piñon were deeply involved in whatever was occurring out there. If Brennan even suspected anything about this, Ladd had no illusions about his own fate.

When the heavy footfalls sounded outside, Abner leaned to haul the door inward and to look through smoke as Lewis Brennan walked inside, faintly scowling. He faced Cass to make his report.

"It's range men from both sides of the road, east and west. There's one hell of a band of broncos raising Cain all around us." He shot Ladd a brief look, then returned his full attention to Cass. "Even back yonder in the lousy mountains."

Walt and Abner straightened up to stare at the constable. Walt in particular had been putting considerable store in their chances of escaping by way of the rearward mountains. Now, he and Abner stared at the lawman.

Brennan did not look very happy either. "The damned Army," he muttered, "drags its butt all over the territory where there aren't no ragheads, and as usual the civilians got to take the bull by the horns."

"That's what all the palavering is about, up at the saloon?" asked Cass, and, when

Brennan inclined his head, Cass rocked forward and leaned both elbows atop the cluttered desk. "Damned good thing they don't have a telegraph here," he dryly said to Walt and Abner, "otherwise by now someone would have telegraphed for the Army."

"The hell with the Army," growled Abner. "That's the least of our worries. Just how do we get out of this damned place?"

"Exactly like we figured to do it," stated Cass, smiling flintily at the younger man. "We'll take our chances with the ragheads up in the mountains. My guess is that, if Buckner's any good at all as a guide, he won't lead us anywhere near a raghead camp. And the reason he won't is because his own darned head will roll if he does. If the ragheads don't waste him, I will." Cass smiled over in Ladd's direction. "What you got to say to that?"

Ladd answered wryly: "Not a hell of a lot. You're right. I don't want to die any more'n the rest of you do."

A man rode slowly up past the jailhouse on a large chestnut horse, his hat tugged low and his shoulders lightly powdered with travel dust. He headed up toward a number of range men and townsmen out front of the saloon in the bright sunlight around one of the tie racks. As Abner leaned to watch, the stranger turned in, stepped off, and, while he was beating dust from his clothing, he spoke in an indistinguishable monotone that seemed to be having a very impressive effect upon his listeners. No one said a word while this stranger was speaking. Afterward, though, there were a number of men with questions, and someone stepped forth to take the reins of the stranger's horse, and also to point southward across the road in the direction of the jailhouse. Abner said: "Hell, he's bein' sent down here." Abner hauled around looking at Cass. "We better lock these bastards into the cells, otherwise this stranger's going to suspect something."

Cass was not excited. "Why lock them up? We're all just having a war council in here, is all. The feller's a stranger, isn't he? Then how would he know we're not plumb legitimate?" Cass motioned. "Take the bar off the door so's he can enter."

Ladd agreed with Cass's logic rather than with the reasoning of Abner, but, when the door finally opened and the stranger walked in to nod around at them all, Ladd's breath stopped in his gullet. The stranger was Joe Reilly!

Lew Brennan, looking more hostile than amiable, said: "What's on your mind, friend?"

Reilly turned a surprised look upon the lawman. He gave the impression of a man who had expected a different kind of greeting. "What's on my mind," Reilly answered curtly, "isn't givin' me the headache I figure it's going to give you, Constable. There is a rampaging band of Apaches plumb around your town, and from what I seen up the stage road behind this place, I'd say they're waiting for nightfall to fire you, then shoot your folks down by the light of their own burning buildings." Reilly gestured with one thick arm. "I was just telling this to some fellers over in front of the saloon and they sure as hell verified for me that there's Indians raidin' all around through here."

Reilly removed his hat and beat more dust from his trousers. Harrison, the saturnine range cattleman, sat staring steadily at Joe Reilly, but he was the only one. As far as Ladd could determine, Reilly's statement, not Reilly the man, had made a deep impression.

Cass stood up from the desk and swore with feeling. Lew Brennan looked ready to slam a big fist into the wall behind him. Abner and Walt turned from Reilly to Cass, but he ignored them completely and paced the room, brows knitted. Twice he stopped to look up the roadway toward the front of the saloon where those townsmen and range men were still clustered in grave conversation. Finally Cass said: "All right, we got to stay, then. That's all there is to it." He turned to Joe Reilly. "Where did you ride from, mister, when you come over here?"

Reilly said: "Piñon, a place south through the. . . ."

"God dammit, I know where Piñon is!" exclaimed the outlaw, and gestured. "Abner, take his damned gun and push him over against the wall with the others."

XIV

Joe Reilly did not resist when he was herded over toward the rear wall, but he gave an excellent imitation of a man who felt indignant over being treated this way when he had gone out of his way to warn of impending Indian trouble. He finally shook clear of Abner and turned fully to face the youthful killer, and to say: "Constable, just what in the hell is the meaning of this? I'm a legitimate traveler on my way through and. . . ."

"Oh, shut up," growled Lewis Brennan. He made it sound enormously disgusted, as though Joe Reilly were the least of his worries, at least the most unimportant of his recent worries.

It was Cass who turned and faced Reilly as he said: "When you was over in Piñon, mister, had they made up a manhuntin' posse to go looking for the fellers who shot up their town and raided their bank?"

"No," said Joe Reilly, staring closely at Cass. "Their lawman was killed in that. . . ." Joe let his voice trail off into silence, and he continued to stare at Cass. When he eventually shifted his attention to the only other armed men in the room excluding the lawman, he said: "You three fellers . . . ?"

No one answered him and Ladd wanted to kick Joe in the shins. Reilly knew perfectly well who Cass, Walt, and Abner were. Going through this moment of mock astonishment was making a nervous wreck of Ladd Buckner.

Walt, who had been silent up to now, gazed a trifle doubtingly at Joe Reilly: "Mister, if those ragheads are all around this town and you was up in the pass yonder . . . how'n hell did you get through and past them to get down here without them cutting you down?"

Reilly smiled. "I saw them," he explained. "I saw them first, and that's nine-tenths of any battle, *amigo*. Once I could see how they were strung out, I only had to make darned certain they didn't look over their shoulders and see me. Then I rode off the roadway and came down through the trees . . . praying every blasted step of the way. It was easy, but by God, mister, I could have died fifty times before I got in among the buildings."

Walt accepted that, probably because it sounded plausible enough. He strolled to the front wall, leaned, and looked out, shook his head, and said: "That's quite a herd of men up in front of the saloon. Why don't they just rig out and get their weapons, and ride out there? If a man can keep ragheads out of the rocks and timber and gullies, he can thin 'em out without much trouble."

Abner sneered: "You and General Custer."

Gradually the men in the jailhouse office lost interest in their latest associate, the man from Piñon, and this allowed Joe to edge over until he was leaning against the same wall Ladd was also leaning against. Joe turned and said: "You got some tobacco, friend?" When Ladd passed over his sack and papers, Reilly methodically went to work.

From a very great distance there came the unmistakable echo of gunshots. It sounded as though there were both carbines and handguns out there. Abner ran through the back of the jailhouse to locate a window and look out there toward the west. Lew Brennan shook his head. "He can't see nothing from back there. There's only one window and it's eight feet from the floor in a cell."

Reilly leaned to return the papers and tobacco sack. "There are no Indians," he whispered swiftly. "It's a scheme to get them out of here." That was all he had time to say as Abner returned, gun in hand as though expecting the Apaches to burst into the jailhouse.

"It was back in them lousy foothills," Abner reported a trifle breathlessly. "You was right, Cass, we das'n't bust out of here tonight and try to make it up into the mountains."

Harrison arose from the chair he had been occupying for a long while and stretched, then turned to gaze from Buckner to Reilly, and smiled. He was still the least anxious individual in the log building. For Ladd, the little bit of information Reilly had been able to give him was enough to convince him that his suspicion about his friends from Piñon being involved in whatever was happening outside the log walls of the Paso jailhouse was correct. But that skimpy information had also aroused a lot more curiosity than it had allayed. Cass, speaking again to Lew Brennan, interrupted Ladd's thoughts.

"What the hell will they do?"

Brennan looked up. "The townsfolk? How would I know?"

As though this were someone's cue, a couple of men from across the road walked over and paused out front to argue a little, then one of them raised a hand as though to knock on the office door, and Cass jerked his head for Brennan to go to the door.

When the lawman pulled back the door and looked out, one of those townsmen said: "Lew, we got a meeting called for fifteen minutes from now over at the saloon. They said we'd better let you know."

Brennan scowled. "What kind of a meeting?"

"Well, damn it," exclaimed the other townsman, looking and sounding aggravated, "what kind of a meeting would folks call when their town's surrounded by a bunch of lousy reservation jumpers? A defense meeting, that's what kind!"

Brennan grumbled and began closing the door. Both those townsmen turned back in the direction of the general store, and Cass, with a bright light in his eye, said something hopeful for the first time in several hours.

"I think we got a way out of here," he said,

and turned. Everyone was staring at him. He saw this, beckoned Walt and Abner to one side, and whispered to them.

Ladd used this moment to hiss a question at Reilly: "Is there a plan?"

Reilly whispered back. "Yes. Get everyone out of here."

"How?"

But before Reilly could risk answering, the three outlaws were ending their little conference. Abner and Walt also looked relieved and hopeful for the first time in hours.

Lew Brennan seemed to be descending deeper into apathy as time passed. When Cass told him it would shortly be time to attend that meeting, Brennan snarled a reply. "There's not a damned thing I can do over there except to advise 'em to either try and bring in troops or try to recruit the range men, then go Indian huntin'. I can darned well tell you one thing. If they put off settling up with those ragheads until after dark, they won't be able to keep them from sneakin' in and firin' the place. If there's one thing ragheads are right good at, it's sneakin' around in the dark."

"Then go tell them that," urged Cass, and went to open the door for Lew Brennan.

Brennan frowned. "They can't get out

onto the range to recruit those cow outfits," he said protestingly. "You heard it . . . the ragheads are completely around us."

Cass accepted this the same way and still held the door. "All right, tell them that, but go attend their meeting."

Cass gestured for Brennan to leave. Ladd guessed this was part of whatever scheme Cass had come up with. He did not want the lawman in the jailhouse. That didn't make much sense, but then Ladd had spent the entire morning thus far listening to things that hadn't made much sense. Brennan stalked out and Cass closed the door behind him.

Reilly leaned and whispered: "One less. Did you ever see one of these log buildings burn?"

Ladd turned and stared, but he had no opportunity to do more than that because Cass called his name.

"Buckner! You know this country so good and you're so sure you can elude the ragheads . . . you ready to go?"

Ladd did not have to pretend to be surprised. "In this damned daylight?"

Cass smiled. "Right now, in this damned daylight. The town's scairt to death over the raghead scare, and somewhere out yonder the Apaches are lying in wait. Well, if we can get out of this jailhouse and over close to the foothills, when dusk falls we'd ought to have good horses and a fair chance of making it." Cass pointed. "It was that traveler gave me the idea. Look at him! Hell, if someone like that can slip through past the Indians, so can we."

None of this was very complimentary to Joe Reilly, but he did not appear to heed the implied insult; he seemed instead to be trying to make some kind of mental adjustment. Perhaps his problem was to try and correlate the outlaw's scheme with some other scheme being perfected by the townsmen. Either way, Ladd Buckner was required to answer Cass. He said: "All right, but I don't like trying this in broad daylight."

Cass was blunt. "You don't have to like anything. All you got to do is lead the way."

It was the range cattleman who broke in to offer an opinion. "The Indians will be watching the town, and the townsmen will be watching the outlying countryside. Mister, you got to be crazy to try something like this."

Cass did not flare up as he had done at other times when his judgment had been challenged. In fact, he continued to smile as he said: "Well, now, cowboy, there is a little more to this. You and that feller who just rode into town this morning, and Buckner there, will be our hostages. If we got to take a few more, we'll do that, too. We're going to walk the bunch of you ahead of us on foot, while we ride, and the townsmen won't dare raise a gun because, if they do, we'll shoot you fellers in the back, one at a time. And the ragheads won't shoot, neither, until we're closer to them than we are to the town. And that's what you'll be for . . . mister . . . shields. If we can't bust around a handful of Indians and make it up through the trees . . . and, mister, no raghead living would abandon his chances of plundering a whole town just to chase after a handful of outlaws who don't have anything but a sackful of greenbacks."

Cass was proud of his plan. Maybe he had reason to be. Ladd eyed the outlaw leader and decided that Cass, whatever else he might be, was not altogether a fool. He knew human nature, apparently, whether it was inside a brown or a white hide. But there was a lot more risk than Ladd Buckner liked to think about.

Walt said: "What about Brennan?"

"Forget Brennan," replied Cass. "That's why I sent him away. He still figures to get the rest of the percentage we owe him."

Cass turned to lean and look out into the empty sun-bright roadway. When he straightened back around, he was still smiling. He drew his Colt and gestured with it toward the back door of the jailhouse office, and, while Walt and Abner stepped back there to lift down the door bar, Cass kicked open the locked lower drawer of the constable's desk to get the sealed bank pouch. Ladd and Joe Reilly exchanged a look, then Joe shrugged thick shoulders and headed in the direction of the doorway. Harrison also turned, looking either resigned or philosophic, and shuffled toward the back wall.

Now that Cass was out of his state of thraldom he was a different person. "Down the back alley," he commanded, "to the rear entrance of the livery barn. We'll take our own animals, if we can't find anything better." He rested his right palm upon the holstered Colt and eyed Ladd a trifle skeptically. "I sure hope you know those mountains," he quietly said.

Ladd didn't know the mountains. He'd never even seen those mountains until he'd crossed through them miles to the west where he'd come up out of one of their cañons to ride into the middle of an Apache bushwhack.

Cass gestured. "Open the door and look

up and down the alleyway, Walt, then let's get to moving."

Abner had his six-gun cocked in his hand. He seemed to think in terms of drawing and cocking his gun regardless of the situation. Cass had to warn him to ease down the hammer, but apparently Cass knew how useless it would also be to tell Abner to holster the gun.

Walt pulled back and nodded. "Nothing in sight either way. Want me to lead off, Cass?"

The outlaw leader nodded his head. Ladd got the impression that Cass would probably have sent Walt out first even if Walt hadn't volunteered. Cass viewed the older outlaw as entirely expendable.

XV

Reilly managed to slip in close beside Ladd and say one thing before Cass and Abner, herding along Harrison and carrying the money pouch, stepped through the doorway into the sun-bright and totally empty alleyway. "The whole damned town is watching."

Ladd had sweat running under his shirt and he hadn't even been out in the sunshine yet. Paso was still too quiet. Whether Cass realized this or not, Ladd did. Each time they passed a building on either side that had daylight showing between it and the next structure, Ladd's breathing became shallow. It was in such places that armed men usually waited.

Nothing happened. There were no armed men in sight. There was only a dog scouting up trash barrels in the alley that looked at them, and, after a moment of picking up impressions, tucked his tail and whisked from sight around a warped wooden corner. The livery barn was southward a few hundred yards. There were three empty lots interspersed here and there along Main Street. They may have attested to the lack of enthusiasm on the part of investors in Paso, but right at this particular moment their value to the men in the alleyway was beyond question. They allowed a clear sighting of Main Street, the east side of it where the store fronts loomed, stolid and empty, and the dusty roadway that was also empty. Abner, still carrying his six-gun loosely on the right side, looked out there, then grinned at Cass and continued to walk along.

"Everybody's up at the saloon." Abner chuckled.

Walt said nothing and kept his eyes swinging from side to side. Clearly this kind of thing was nothing new to the oldest outlaw, and just as clearly he was right now functioning at his best.

Ladd used a cuff to push sweat off his forehead. It was one thing to be armed and in trouble and something altogether different to be in trouble and unarmed.

Joe Reilly reached inside his coat vigorously to scratch. His gaze at Ladd was humorous and sardonic. Evidently Reilly had decided that whether he survived this ordeal or not, he was not going to start praying until he had to.

Harrison, the range cowman, usually had a brown-paper cigarette dangling from his thin lips and this moment was no exception. He looked from left to right, cigarette dangling without being lighted, and, when Cass turned and their glances crossed, the cowman drawled an opinion. "You might have it figured right at that. Everyone is so busy worrying about everyone else, you just might make it. Your worst danger'll be beyond town."

Cass answered almost pleasantly. "Yeah, problem will be slipping around the ragheads, but being in the forest, and knowing they're out there and they won't know we're out there, ought to make a difference." Cass continued to gaze at Harrison. "How far's your ranch from here?"

"Four miles due west along the foothills until you come to a big washout in the roadway where a creek comes down, then due north from there another couple of miles. Why? You want to go to work on a cow outfit?"

"If we got to run for shelter out of the mountains," explained Cass, "I want to know where to run to."

Harrison accepted this. "All right. If you can make it to the ranch, you'll be plenty safe. I bought the outfit from a Mex family that built it. The main house and the bunk-house got walls three feet thick and barred windows. You can sit in there and eat a nice pleasant supper with all the Indians on earth trying to get at you from the yard. They can't even burn it."

Walt made a little trilling sound of warning up ahead. Everyone slackened pace to look. A large, thick, ugly man had just walked indifferently from the rear of the livery barn and was now standing down there in the center of the alley, legs wide, hands on hips, staring up at the group of men walking toward him. As near as could be determined, the man in the center of the alley was unarmed, but he had the truculent appearance of an individual who, guns or no guns, would be disagreeable if he chose to be, and perhaps this kind of attitude arose from the man's size and build; he was large and massive and layered with powerful muscles. His face showed the scars of many brawls, and, when he turned aside to spit amber, his neck muscles were like steel cables.

Walt kept right on walking. When he was less than a hundred feet from the burly, beetle-browed individual, old Walt simply drew and cocked his six-gun, and those two were suddenly complete equals. In fact, old Walt, who could have stood behind the big man without any part of him showing, had the advantage.

The big man looked surprised, then he spat again, and removed his hands from his hips, and that helped a little; at least now he did not look as though he wanted to fight the whole crowd of them.

Walt gestured. "Inside the barn, mister, and just walk nice and easy."

Abner had his gun cocked again, but this time Cass offered no admonition.

The barn's cool, shaded runway had been freshly raked and watered down. The big man turned, finally, to chew his cud in speculative thought as he studied the motley crew in front of him.

Walt said: "You the day man, friend?"

The big man nodded. "Yeah, what do you want?"

Walt smiled and tilted up his gun barrel. "The best strong young horses you got, friend, without no trouble."

The liveryman spat again, looked over Walt's head and Abner's head to Cass, who he had instinctively singled out as spokesman, and said: "Help yourself. But I'm not goin' to lift a hand to help you steal 'em."

From the corner of his eye Ladd saw Abner's gun hand begin to rise. "I've yet to see the horse I'd die over," he told the liveryman, and by this remark drew the hostler's attention to Abner and the look on his face as his gun hand continued to rise. Ladd could do no more.

The day man struggled with himself, and in the end just as Abner's cocked gun settled to bear, the hostler turned with a curse and pointed. "In them yonder stalls on the south wall, gents, is four of the best animals around Paso. They been raced a little, though, so you'd better know how to set a horse." He dropped his arm and turned. "Saddles, bridles, and blankets are behind me in the harness room."

Cass looked at Ladd. "You just saved that

feller's life," he said quietly, and turned to study the day man again, and also to say: "And I can tell you right now, Buckner, he's a bully and a lot worse, and there'll be folks around town who'd just as soon see him get shot." Cass for once seemed on the verge of approving a murder, but instead of allowing Abner to kill the big hostler, Cass showed contempt in his voice when he said: "Step inside, mister, pick out the outfits Abner'll show you, and haul 'em out here. You try to get a gun from a drawer or a saddlebag in there, and Abner'll gut-shoot you with my blessing."

Abner waited. When the day man turned to obey, Abner smiled at Cass as though grateful for this opportunity to kill a man. It made Ladd Buckner's hair stand on end. To one side of him Joe Reilly, who had not had much opportunity to make personal assessments, now watched Abner stroll away with special interest.

The liveryman had evidently also guessed all he had to know because he returned almost at once burdened with two saddles, then he wordlessly and briskly returned for another saddle and the blankets and bridles. For a person whose truculence had been noticeable halfway up the alleyway, he had made a rather complete metamorphosis. He

still looked bleak and he watched the outlaws closely, but he was careful to give no
offence.

Ladd had a chance to get over beside Joe
Reilly when Walt stepped ahead to lend the
hostler a hand, and while Abner watched
them both as he and Cass stood side-by-
side, conversing in near whispers.

Ladd asked if they might have been seen
abandoning the jailhouse. Joe's whispered
reply was curt. "You can bet on it. They're
all around the place. By now they'll be all
around this end of town."

"Will they let us leave?"

Reilly put a sardonic look upon his friend
and shook his head just once, very emphati-
cally.

Walt swore at a tall black gelding they
were rigging out and the gelding stopped
fidgeting, but now he rolled his eyes.

Abner was sent up to the front of the barn
to look over the town and the northward
roadway. To Ladd this seemed like an excellent moment for the townsmen to storm the
barn. But it did not happen that way.

Cass, who never once allowed either of his
companions to carry the sack with the
money pouch inside it, turned toward Harrison, the cowman, with a question. "You
know those mountains, too?"

Harrison replied judiciously. "I've hunted 'em a little, and I've rode after lost livestock up in there a few times."

"You'll know whether we can out-sly the damned Apaches, then," replied the outlaw leader. "You walk up ahead with Buckner."

Cass turned his back on the captives again as Abner returned to report that there was no more sign of life now than there had been a couple of hours earlier. "It's plumb unnatural for a town to be this quiet," he warned. "Hell, there's only a couple of range riders up in front of the saloon, and a feller across the road out front working on the wheel of someone's freight rig in front of the blacksmith's place."

Abner, getting no acknowledgment, turned beside Cass to watch the saddling process. He had holstered his Colt for a change.

A man whistled out back in the alleyway, which brought the outlaws around in a blur of drawn weapons and apprehension, but the whistler was making no secret of his advance and in fact the tune he was whistling was a very popular one called "Gerryowen." It was the tune Custer's 7th Cavalry had favored on their long march to oblivion on the Little Big Horn. It was also popular among saloon patrons; scarcely a Saturday night went by in most cow towns that someone with a mouth organ, a banjo, or even a jew's-harp didn't liven up the comradeship and the drinking by playing it.

The outlaws did not come out of their crouches or lower their guns, although, as the whistler approached, it became increasingly evident that he had no intention of trying to sneak up on anyone. Then he rounded the doorway from out back and Ladd recognized Constable Lew Brennan. So also did everyone else including the burly hostler who seemed to be of half a mind to draw encouragement from the appearance of Paso's lawman. Clearly the hostler like most other people in town did not as yet realize the extent of the perfidy of their town constable.

But Brennan did not keep the hostler long in doubt. As he walked forward and as the outlaws were hauling back up out of their fighting stances, Brennan said: "Cass, by God, you deliberately tried to get rid of me so's you fellers could leave town."

Cass shrugged. "If you mean because we didn't figure to take you along . . . that's right, Constable."

"I mean," averred the angry lawman, "you figured to beat me out of that money you owe me. You lied about how much you got

160

down at Piñon so's you wouldn't have to come up with my full percentage. Then you was going to ride out. That's why you sent me to that damned meeting."

Cass said nothing. He gazed at Lew Brennan with completely dispassionate regard, then turned and nodded at Abner. Without any warning Abner drew and fired. Ladd was just as astonished as was Reilly and the hostler, as was the lawman who took that slug hard, high in the body. Ladd glimpsed the expression of pure surprise that flashed for seconds over Brennan's face, then the lawman went down backward, struck wood, and rolled into the center of the runway, dead.

Abner's gunshot acted as a signal. From far up the runway and out across the roadway where that jacked-up freight wagon was parked in front of the blacksmith's shop, four men pushed off a tarp, raised up, shoved rifles over the sideboard, and fired a ragged volley. No one inside the barn was expecting this, but they all reacted the same way by frantically trying to hurl themselves into the nearest shadows.

Abner paused to fire back, face twisted into a murderous expression. The men prone in the wagon bed fired another ragged volley. Abner's gun went off into the overhead air, and from the alleyway out back someone yelled at him. Abner tried to turn and another ragged volley cut him down and rolled him in the dirt.

XVI

Joe Reilly had called the shots when he had told Ladd the outlaws would not be allowed to leave Paso, but now that the fight had started Ladd had a moment to wonder if those townsmen would allow anyone else, including the hostages to survive, either. Bullets came down through the barn from across the front roadway, and out back several men on either side of the big door-less opening also fired up through. The wonder was not that Abner had been riddled to death; the wonder was that everyone else hadn't also been riddled including the terrified big black horse wearing a saddle but no bridle, as it wildly snorted and charged out the back of the barn and beyond town.

Ladd had been careful to go with Joe Reilly when everyone scattered. They crouched inside an empty horse stall, listening to the gunfire. During a brief pause Joe said: "The whole darned town's mobilized. Simon and Doc and I saw to that when you didn't return from the jailhouse. We figured something had gone bad wrong up there. One or two folks around town told us Brennan wasn't considered to be above helping outlaws hide, for a price."

Ladd had no time to comment. The gunfire started up again, but there was nothing he had to tell Joe Reilly about Paso's dishonest lawman. In fact, there would be no point in talking about Brennan to anyone from now on. Paso could bury him and that would be that. There were only two outlaws still alive in the livery barn, but, as Ladd learned to differentiate between gunfire outside the building and gunfire emanating from inside it, he was impressed at the defense Walt and Cass were putting up. Then all the gunfire from outside ended very suddenly and a man's bull-toned voice sang out from the roadway.

"Hey, you boys in the barn, listen to me! You aren't going out of there except you come out hands high or except you come out feet first. We agreed to give you this one chance to surrender. What'll it be?"

The answer was a gunshot in the direction from which that voice had come. It was something done in frank defiance only, since no one could see the man who had spoken. Now, when Ladd and Joe braced for more wild gunfire, only two riflemen took up the fight, one in front, one out back.

Ladd listened and Joe Reilly said: "Don't think for a minute all they got over here is clods. There's a feller works at the general store who was badly wounded in the war who was a full colonel. He's directing things. Right now he's using his sharpshooters. Simon and Doc and I sat in on their war council and this feller took command. Believe me, those outlaws don't stand a single blessed chance."

"If they were smart, they'd give up," Ladd said, but Reilly shook his head.

"Too late."

"You mean that man meant it. They aren't going to let Cass and Walt give up?"

Joe was emphatic. "They said they'd give 'em one chance, and after that they'd bore in until they'd killed every blasted one of them."

Ladd listened to the gunfire. It was more like a duel between two men with rifles or carbines, and two other men with six-guns, and that was exactly what it was. First one side would fire, then the other side would retaliate, but the riflemen seemed repeatedly to change position while the pair of outlaws inside the livery barn remained stationary. What ultimately broke up this duel was someone with a shotgun firing from inside the barn. The noise was not just deafening; it also was followed by the splintering of wood and the loud cursing of a man Ladd thought was Walt.

For a moment only the ear-ringing echoes lingered, then two six-guns blazed away, and this time they were firing at something inside the barn. Again the shotgun went off, first one deafening barrel, then the other deafening barrel. A man cried out, a pair of simultaneous six-guns blazed back, and Ladd joined Joe Reilly in crawling belly down to the doorway of their horse stall to peek around.

That bully day man was lying face down over along the opposite side of the runway, the shotgun still in a grip of one scarred big fist. The townsmen beyond the barn were suddenly silent, listening and trying to guess what had happened. Harrison, the cowman, utilized this moment to sing out: "Cass, you're done for." It was said in his customarily calm and casual tone. "Did you see Walt? He's caught one of those full-bore blasts in the chest. You can read a newspaper through him, and that means you're all that's left. Cass . . . ?"

There was no answer or any more defiant gunfire. Joe screwed up his face. "He's hit sure as hell, and maybe he's even dead," Joe whispered to Ladd. "Which stall was he in?"

Ladd had no idea. When they had all initially scattered in panic, the only person Ladd had kept an eye upon was Reilly.

"Can you see around the door?" Joe asked.

Ladd inched ahead a little, until he saw the dead lawman and Abner, then he squeezed over closer and craned harder until he could also see up past the harness room where the dead day man was lying, still gripping his shotgun, all the way to the front roadway. There was no one to be seen and there was no noise. He pulled back. "Three corpses and that's all," he reported.

Reilly, upon the opposite side of their stall opening, also inched ahead and sought to look out and around in the opposite direction. Without warning someone fired, a long pale splinter of stall door wood took flight, and the door itself was slammed back hard against Reilly, almost stunning him, but instinct made him back-pedal as swiftly as he could. Ladd thought Joe had been hit until the saloon man pointed to the splintered stall door.

A man said — "I know which stall he's in." — and followed this up by firing into the siding of the stall where Joe and Ladd were crouching.

Horse stalls were usually built of planking

that would resist the normal abuse animals might give, but they were never built to withstand gunfire. The siding that was protecting Reilly and Buckner stopped a number of slugs and turned aside more slugs, but it was also gradually disintegrating until Ladd decided, if he continued to lie there, he and Joe Reilly were going to be killed, and pulled back as far as he could into a corner, then waited for the gunfire to pause, so that he might make a dash for some other place of concealment.

The lull arrived when Paso's townsmen decided they surely must have obliterated someone inside that shot-up horse stall, but just as Ladd was rising to run, someone in a stall up closer to the front roadway fired twice, very fast, and over among the men in the freight wagon a man cried out in pain. Now, those men in the alleyway saw their mistake. They shifted their sights and began systematically blazing away at the stall where Cass had fired from. Reilly motioned for Ladd to get back down flat again, and in this position they heard someone running toward their stall and were absolutely helpless to do anything about it. They hadn't even heard the man running until he was so close they had no time to jump up and face him.

It was Harrison, the range cowman, and he was clutching that shotgun the day man had died firing. As he sprang inside and saw the pair of men lying prone inside, he swung the shotgun for a moment, then swung it away, and sank to one knee as he said: "I think I can nail him from here."

Before either Joe or Ladd could speak, Harrison knelt in the doorway and raised his shotgun to rest on the door top. After a moment without the exposed shotgun barrel drawing gunfire from the outlaw leader up front, Harrison slowly raised up to snug back the shotgun as though it were a rifle, and aim it.

That was when the six-gun blast came without warning and Harrison went down backward and rolled in agony, his shotgun falling close to Ladd in the straw. Without a moment of reflection Ladd grabbed the weapon and jumped over to the edge of the door, but low enough so that he would come around it from the floor. He looked up as soon as he was exposed. Cass was just lowering himself again. Ladd fired even though he felt certain it was too late.

Wood burst up where Cass had been and a man's clear-toned profanity erupted up there. Ladd hauled back the second hammer and waited. Cass did not make an attempt to fire back, and he did not expose himself, but Ladd had accomplished something the dozen or so men out front had most earnestly hoped for and that none of them had been able to accomplish. Ladd pulled the outlaw leader's full attention away from the roadway, which allowed those men out there to get realigned. One of them suddenly leaned around the doorless front opening and fired on the spur of the moment. The bullet raked the paneling one foot from Ladd. He dived back inside his cell where Joe Reilly was working over the wounded cattleman. Neither Harrison nor Joe glanced up as the gunfire became brisk again.

Ladd waited. He had one more loaded barrel in his scatter-gun so he could not join in any indiscriminate shoot-outs. He waited, listening and estimating and deciding what his chances might be. When there was another lull, he eased to the broken door again, eased around it to peer in the direction of Cass's horse stall, and from out back in the alley a man yelled at him.

"Get the hell out of the way, Buckner!"

Ladd glanced over his shoulder. Simon, the Piñon blacksmith, was down there holding a long-barreled rifle in both hands.

Ladd turned his back on Simon. Up

ahead Cass fired into the roadway again. Ladd knew what he would do, finally. He waited until the townsmen had got Cass to fire back at them again, then Ladd stood up and moved swiftly on the balls of his feet. He had about ten or twelve yards to traverse before he could look down into the horse stall which was his objective. He heard someone out back sharply commanding someone else not to shoot. Otherwise, he did not feel especially exposed, although there was no doubt about it, he was not just exposed, he was also unknown to most of the townsmen out there, waiting. He was in the most dangerous situation of his lifetime when he stalked the deadly outlaw leader up in one of those front stalls.

Simon had made certain those townsmen out back would not fire at Ladd. Out front, over in the freight wagon where the wounded man was still groaning, Dr. Orcutt was not just working on the injured man; he was also explaining to the townsmen around him and within hearing distance of his voice who that whisking shadow was, down there in the runway.

Ladd only knew he was close enough to Cass's horse stall to raise his shotgun. He could not risk a snap shot. He had only one blast in the old weapon, and, if he missed with it, or if he wasted it, he was going to pay with his life. He knew it. He had never thought of Cass as any less of a murderer than Abner had been. He began to rise up just outside of Cass's stall. Inside, since no one was firing at him, Cass was down on his knees, reloading. As it turned out, this was the last time he would be able to reload; he had shot out all the extra shells from his shell belt. One way or another, Cass had come to the end of his personal trail.

Ladd kept rising up. When he was able to do it, he lifted the scatter-gun in both hands, then began the final maneuver that would permit him to lift the shotgun over the half wall of the stall. As he did this, the man in there on his knees caught sight of a shadow from the corner of his eyes and with incredible speed slammed closed the gate of his Colt and twisted from the waist, simultaneously tipping up the Colt barrel. Ladd had the shotgun pushed straight ahead when he pulled the trigger. That blast, in such a confined place, sounded like a Howitzer being fired, and the full bore of that scatter-gun charge lifted Cass half to his feet and hurled him violently back into the far wall, then allowed him slowly to fold forward and slide off the wall, dead.

XVII

Enos Orcutt had six wounded individuals, which was somewhat of a surprise to Ladd and Joe Reilly. The only wounded men they were aware of were two in number; one of them was over in the freight wagon out front of the blacksmith's shop, and they had heard that man cry out when Cass had shot him, while the other injured one was that cattleman, Harrison, and he had been less than ten feet from them when he had been hit. Otherwise, though, they'd seen no one get hit and hadn't really thought much about this possibility except when the townsmen had mistakenly opened up and had splintered the front wall of the stall they had been hiding in.

Now that it was over, Ladd walked back to the stall where Joe Reilly was still working over Harrison. Until now Ladd hadn't even seen Harrison's wound, which was through the left shoulder up high and may not have broken any bones. Ladd pitched something into the straw near Joe. It was the sack with the money pouch inside it. Joe looked over, looked up at Ladd, and said: "You get the son-of-a-bitch?"

Ladd nodded. "How's Harrison?"

Reilly looked down. "He needs Enos.

You'd better go out there and find him."

"Mind the money," Ladd said, and leaned the scatter-gun aside as he turned to leave the barn. Out front there were several visible armed men for a change. Everyone seemed to realize it was over. Ladd called across to the men around the wagon.

"Is Doctor Orcutt over there?"

He was, and he'd just completed giving instructions to the injured man's brother for the care of that man Cass had wounded in the wagon. He turned and strode across, accompanied by several armed townsmen. When he got close, he looked closely at Ladd before saying: "You hit, by any chance?"

"No. Joe and I made it through all right, but there's a cowman in the stall with Joe who got hit . . . Enos?"

Orcutt paused to say: "Six injured ones counting your cowman, Ladd . . . Cass and Walt and Abner?"

"Dead in there. You'll see them." Ladd felt tired and drawn out. "I'll be at the bath-house if anyone needs me," he added, and turned to walk away. Enos Orcutt barked at a couple of townsmen who started after Buckner.

"Leave him alone for a while," the doctor said.

The town was beginning to show new signs of life as Ladd approached the jailhouse, then walked right on past it all the way up to the rooming house where he got the key to the bathhouse, plus a towel and a chunk of lye soap from a teen-aged boy who couldn't fathom someone wanting to bathe at a time like this, when three notorious bank robbers were holed up down at the livery barn, fighting it out with the entire town, plus several men from over at Piñon. Ladd listened to all the youth had to say, nodded, and walked out back to the one place in Paso, aside from private dwellings, where a body could get a decent bath. He was also hungry, but that consideration could wait.

By the time he was freshly attired and smelling strongly of lye soap, Paso had assessed the cost of its unexpected, savage fight. There was no undertaker in Paso, but the proprietor of the general store, the only person in town who owned a sawdust-filled icehouse, allowed the dead to be stacked in his icehouse until other dispositions could be arranged for.

There were still people who had difficulty grasping the fact that Constable Lewis Brennan had not only been killed, but had also been in league with outlaws. On the other hand there were enough other people around the Paso countryside who suspected that Brennan had never been a man of purest virtue. As Harrison was to say later, when he was able to be up and around: "Maybe they sometimes start out plumb honest, but after a few years in office . . . providin' they was raised by folks who themselves never could make out the difference between real right and wrong . . . they just sort of slide right down to the renegade level."

Ladd Buckner and his companions from Piñon did not hear Harrison say that because by the time the cowman was able to be up and around, the men from Piñon had been back home for a week or so.

On the ride back, with Joe Reilly in charge of the money sack, it was the taciturn blacksmith who made the most cryptic observation. "Two days wasted, damned near killed a dozen times, got the money that don't belong to none of us, and now we go home to hand it over to folks who'll never understand all we went through to get it back for 'em. Why?"

Dr. Orcutt, looking more raffish than ever in his tipped-back dented derby, his torn and rumpled and soiled frock coat, and his unshaven countenance, replied with a twinkle: "Simon, you do things without thinking because you know without thinking you should do them. If any of us had coldly thought this thing through, we wouldn't any of us have struck out like we did. Emotionalism gets people killed every day, but even when they are dead, they are still better men than the ones who react coldly and avoid their responsibilities." Doc glanced at the blacksmith. "How's that for being profound when I need a bath, a shave, and probably protection from the folks in Piñon who'll be mad as hornets about me traipsing off to play lawman?"

Reilly fished in a saddle pocket and brought forth a bottle of brandy. "Got it free in Paso," he said, offering it around. Doc took two swallows and Simon Terry had three swallows, but neither Reilly nor Buckner took a drop.

They were coming down the near side of the pass and could distantly make out roof tops and sun-brightened glass windowpanes even from that distance, when the south-bound coach headed for Piñon, after having briefly stopped back in Paso, careered past, stirring dust to high heaven and forcing the men from Piñon to the shoulder of the road where they cursed the driver with considerable feeling.

"He can't wait to get down to Piñon to tell all he knows," growled Dr. Orcutt. "They never get anything right."

Joe Reilly had vindicated himself honorably, had resolved what he would have classified as his civic responsibility, and now was perfectly free to think in other terms. He therefore said: "Lads, when we get back and you've had a little time to clean up and get straight again, drop by the saloon this evening. You'll be deserving all the free likker the boys'll want to pour down you to hear the lurid and true story of all we've gone through in the interests of law 'n' order."

Ladd, remembering that his background had been exposed, pointed to the sack tied to Reilly's saddle horn. "Just you be damned certain you get that pouch back to the folks at the bank. And not tonight. The minute you get back to town."

Joe looked aggrieved. "That was my intention right from the start."

Doc smiled at Simon and the blacksmith did not smile back. He simply looked dead ahead, already thinking of the work he had to do, starting fresh tomorrow.

ABOUT THE AUTHOR

Lauran Paine who, under his own name and various pseudonyms has written over a thousand books, was born in Duluth, Minnesota. His family moved to California when he was at a young age and his apprenticeship as a Western writer came about through the years he spent in the livestock trade, rodeos, and even motion pictures where he served as an extra because of his expert horsemanship in several films starring movie cowboy Johnny Mack Brown. In the late 1930s, Paine trapped wild horses in northern Arizona and even, for a time, worked as a professional farrier. Paine came to know the Old West through the eyes of many who had been born in the previous century, and he learned that Western life had been very different from the way it was portrayed on the screen. "I knew men who had killed other men," he later recalled. "But they were the exceptions. Prior to and during the Depression, people were just too busy eking out an existence to indulge in Saturday-night brawls." He served in the U.S. Navy in the Second World War and began writing for Western pulp magazines following his discharge. It is interesting to note that all of his earliest novels (written under his own name and the pseudonym Mark Carrel) were published in the British market and he soon had as strong a following in that country as in the United States. Paine's Western fiction is characterized by strong plots, authenticity, an apparently effortless ability to construct situation and character, and a preference for building his stories upon a solid foundation of historical fact. *Adobe Empire* (1956), one of his best novels, is a fictionalized account of the last twenty years in the life of trader William Bent and, in an off-trail way, has a melancholy, bittersweet texture that is not easily forgotten. In later novels like *Cache Cañon* (Five Star Westerns, 1998) and *Halfmoon Ranch* (Five Star Westerns, 2007), he showed that the special magic and power of his stories and characters had only matured along with his basic themes of changing times, changing attitudes, learning from experience, respecting Nature, and the

yearning for a simpler, more moderate way
of life.